Molly and John Burkett

Foxes Three

illustrations by Julie Stiles

Piccolo Pan Books
London and Sydney

First published in Great Britain 1977 by André Deutsch Limited
This edition published 1979 by Pan Books Ltd,
Cavaye Place, London SW10 9PG
© Molly and John Burkett 1975
Illustrations © Julie Stiles 1977
ISBN 0 330 25789 7
Printed in Great Britain by
Richard Clay (The Chaucer Press) Ltd, Bungay, Suffolk

Foxes Three

Molly Burkett and her husband run the Animal Rehabilitation Centre in Lincolnshire. Their children, Sophie and co-author John, are considerably older than they were when the fox cubs arrived, but they still clearly remember the pleasure of looking after the tiny defenceless animals.

Molly Burkett trained as a teacher, and she has written many magazine articles on the care of birds and mammals and the work done at the centre.

this book is dedicated to my
three little foxes,
Gavin, Stephen and Kerry-Ann

chapter one

I wanted to rear a fox cub, but Mum said, 'No.'

Mum and Dad ran a wildlife centre at Hough-on-the-Hill in Lincolnshire where we lived. We had not always lived there. We used to live at Bentworth in Hampshire, but when Dad was offered a job up here we all had to come – us, three hundred birds, animals and all. We even had some birds sitting on eggs when the moving vans turned up and they came up complete. I can never remember a time when we have not had animals and birds that needed to be reared or cared for. Well, I wanted one for myself and I wanted a fox.

I knew that most of our animals went back to the wild when they were fit enough, but we could not always let them go. Sometimes their injuries did not heal and sometimes they did not want to go because they had become too tame. It is cruel to take a tame animal out into the country and leave it there if it has not been taught to look after itself. Sometimes Sophie and I did not want the animals to go because we liked having them.

We had a fox once.

He was a truly wild animal. He would never have become a pet. There was something about his bearing, his alertness, his nobility that got right inside me. This fox had come to us with a broken leg. Dad had taken him to the vet and had it set. It was a bad break and the whole leg had to be plastered. We had fixed him up in the shed, making sure all the windows and doors were shut so that he could not escape before the plaster was off.

We had a heron that did that once. We had had it for nearly four weeks and its plaster was ready to come off its wing. As Dad bent down to pick it up, the bird had simply spread its wings and taken off, flying right over the roof-tops as if there was not a thing wrong with it. We had a real job getting it back. In the end we found it six miles away, and Dad simply took the plaster off where it was and left it there. As Dad said, if it could look after itself with half a wing it ought to manage superbly with all its additions in the right order.

That fox was a magnificent creature, red brown in colour. His pointed mask and ears gave his appearance intelligence and alertness. I thought he was everything that a wild animal should be, and I spent hours watching him. He seemed to appreciate that we were trying to help him and he tolerated us. He never accepted us. When we went in to feed him, the fox would draw back into the corner and watch us. He would sink down on to his haunches, resting his head on his front paws, and look up at us warily. Everything we did, every movement we made was watched unwaveringly by the

animal. He showed no fear at all, just this cautious aware-ness.

We tried never to go towards him. It is much better to allow an animal to come to you, so we would clean him out and change his water and try to pretend he was not there, except that all the time you could feel his eyes looking at you, and when you did glance in his direction your eyes would meet his unwavering look.

Dad had to go up to him sometimes though to make sure that leg was all right and the plaster was not rubbing him sore. The fox did not move, he did not even lift his head as Dad went near, but the look in his eye changed and he growled. It was a low growl that rose from the back of his throat, and it sounded menacing.

Dad is used to handling all sorts of wild animals and he has got himself into one or two tricky situations that way. He stopped when the fox growled like that; even he was not sure of it. He approached the animal very cautiously.

The fox was never at ease when we were in the shed with him, but we found a way round that. I would go in with Dad and then, after a couple of minutes, he would go out and leave me in there. The fox always thought we had both gone out. Foxes may seem intelligent but they cannot count. As soon as the door shut he would shake himself with obvious satisfaction and tuck into his meal with real enjoy-ment, something he would never do when we were watching him.

Despite the plastered leg, he moved with a stealth and arrogance that were wonderful to watch, but he was always alert. If there was any unusual noise, such as a motorbike going up the lane or the children next door shouting, then he would freeze immediately, standing like a statue until it had gone or until he had convinced himself that it did not mean danger. Even when he was sleeping, if there was an unexpected noise, however slight, he would straight away lift his head and look in the direction from which it had

9

come and only settle down again when it had passed.

That fox fascinated me. There was something in his bearing that I had never seen before, the nobility, the arrogance of a truly wild animal perfectly content in its own world and prepared to accept ours for a short while because circumstances had made it necessary. It showed in the way he moved, his reaction when disturbed, his awareness of things around him, his tolerance of the situation in which he found himself. He was always aware, cautious, prepared.

The day the vet removed the plaster from his leg, we left the door of the shed open. Mum had wanted us to take the fox right up into the woods and let him go there because she thought he would stay around and frighten all the other animals and even start killing them. Dad said we need not bother about that; as soon as the fox smelled freedom he would be as far away from Hough-on-the-Hill as he could possibly get.

I sat and watched the shed door. I wanted to see him go. I told myself I wanted to make sure the leg had mended all right, but I knew it had. I really wanted to see the animal in his own environment, see how he would look against a natural backcloth of grass and sky, to have a last look at him. I sat there waiting for him to come out for the best part of an hour. There was not a sign of him and I began to get impatient. It was not working out as I had expected. I thought I would have seen the proud animal trotting off over the hill with that graceful, flowing yet purposeful movement that a fox has. I went across to the shed to see what he was doing.

He was not there.

I could hardly believe it. I turned over the straw and looked in the box, but he had gone. I could have sworn that I had not taken my eyes from that shed door all the while I had been waiting, but he had gone so stealthily I had not even seen a shadow.

chapter two

Whatever Mum said, I was determined that one day I would have a fox cub for myself. I knew it would not be a truly wild creature like the one with the broken leg that we had cared for, but at least it would have some of the nobility and some of the cunning that that animal had shown, and it would be mine.

Mum seemed equally determined that I was not going to have one. 'You want an animal for the wrong reason,' she said. 'It's like a small child wanting a toy, and an animal is not a toy, especially a wild one like a fox. It's entitled to its own way of life, and anything you offer it would only be a substitute. Besides, you've got to be sensible. A fox is one animal we can do without here. What would happen if it got out? Nothing would be safe, none of the birds at any rate, not even the old swan. Foxes are killers. They'll kill anything that moves. It's part of their nature. They're not like badgers and otters that only kill when they're hungry.'

When the fox cubs did turn up there was not much she could do about it though.

The phone call came out of the blue. Sophie and I were watching a film on television when Dad shouted at us to turn the sound down. He could not hear what someone was saying on the phone. So we turned it down and went on watching people moving across the screen like a modern ballet, and we had to imagine what they might have been saying. Dad's voice intruded on the quietness, and then it gradually dawned on me what he was saying and all thought of the film went out of my mind immediately.

We heard Dad say, 'Of course I'll take them, although I must admit they're the one animal I'm never keen to have.

They're so difficult to release, and it's hard to find a spot to let them go where they're not likely to be hunted. By the time the young ones are ready to go, the hunt are out cubbing, and if yours have got tame at all they're as likely to run up to the hounds as away from them.'

'Someone's bringing a fox in,' Sophie said.

I was out in the hall straight away and waiting for Dad to put that phone down. The film was not important after all. Dad reckoned he had not mentioned the word 'fox'; in fact he said he could not remember what he had been talking about.

'You did, you did, you did,' Sophie chanted at him.

In the end he told us about the fox cubs. There was not one; there were three. A farmer had dug them out from beneath his chicken house. He did not want to keep them but he did not want them killed, so he had phoned up a friend of Dad's who used to look after animals in the same way that we do now. This friend had had to give it all up when his wife was taken ill, so he phoned Dad up to ask if he could help. Dad's friend said he was bringing them right over and he was with us within an hour. It was obvious from the way he looked at those three little animals lying there in the basket that he would have liked to keep them himself. In the end we promised him that if ever he found himself in a position to keep animals again we would let him have one of those foxes back.

When he had gone I sat on the floor beside the basket and looked at those tiny creatures. We had to keep them in the bathroom because it was the only room we had that had a thermostat-controlled heater. This meant we could keep them in a constant temperature. We had a huge laundry basket in which someone had once sent us an eagle with a broken wing. It had been temporary 'home' to countless things since then, and the fox cubs were added to the end of the list. We had cleaned and disinfected it and filled it with hay, and the cubs filled the tiny depression in the middle.

I felt a bit disappointed. I had wanted a fox cub for so long, and now that I had three in my possession, well, they did not look like small foxes at all, more like mongrel puppies. I could see no similarity between them and the magnificent dog fox that I had loved to watch.

These three had dull chocolate brown coats and their ears were soft and rounded. It was obvious that they had been dug out, because they were all muddy and one of them had a grazed nose and a little bit out of one ear. Their muzzles were soft and pink and their pale blue eyes were weak and seemed incapable of focusing on anything. The smallest of the three still had its eyelids drawn down over the greater part of its eyes.

'They're only about ten days old,' Dad said, looking down at them. 'I should think their eyes had only just opened.'

The biggest one of the three chose that moment to begin crying. It did not sound like the call of a wild thing at all. The cub mewed like a little kitten, and all the time it was scrabbling upward until it was climbing over the other two.

Sophie decided it was hungry, but Dad said we must give them time to settle down, because everything would be strange to them and the journey by car could not have done them any good. He put the lid down on the basket, and we quietly left them on their own.

We had to push the dogs out of the way to get out of the bathroom. It was most peculiar. They were both used to animals and never bothered anything that was brought into the centre, but these fox cubs, young as they were, had a really odd effect on them. Both of the dogs were going frantic to get in to them.

We had two dogs, a little whippet we called Puppy although she had been two years old when she came to us, and Susie, a spaniel. We had lost Tessa, our old English setter. She had picked up some poison when she had been out over the fields with me. I could hardly believe she was dead. She had shared so much of my life. I suppose Sophie and I should have understood death a bit, being brought up in a centre where our parents deal with sick and injured creatures. It stands to reason that some of them are going to die. In a way we have learned to accept death, but that did not help when Tessa died.

We said we would never have another dog; we were all upset and knew that nothing could ever replace her. When I came home from school the very next day, there was Puppy. Somebody had asked Mum if she would take her because their other whippet kept on turning on her. She was one of the sweetest-natured little dogs that we have ever known, always alert and always affectionate. As far as possible she slipped into the space that Tessa had left. Yet there was a side of her, a wildness that would suddenly assert itself, and for a short while we would see a side of her nature that was at complete variance to the one we had come to love.

Tessa had run off from time to time, especially if there had been a hare for her to chase, and then she would not come when we called her. But you could see her trying not to hear us; she knew we had called her and she did not want to come. When she did come back she would look sad and sorry because she knew she had done wrong. Puppy was different. She would run off with speed and directness, and it seemed that she could not help herself. She just ran and ran. We would call her but it seemed that she was unable to hear us. If she could not run in a straight line she ran round and round, jumping up at anyone that got in her way. She got into a chicken run once when she was in that mood, and the farmer lost thirty hens. Whether they had panicked and rushed against the wire or whether Puppy had snapped at them, we never did decide, but Dad had a stiff bill to settle.

These moods were rare. They started and stopped without warning. Most of the time she was gentle and obedient and she followed me everywhere like a shadow. She came over the fields with me, and when I went out on my bike, she followed so closely behind my back wheel that the policeman thought I had her on a leash behind me. She even used to follow me when I went to bed. When Mum was not looking, Puppy would jump and wriggle right down under the bedclothes and lie on my feet. Mum was always grumbling about the state of my feet. She insisted I never washed them, because the sheets were always so dirty, but it was Puppy's fault, not mine.

I had to stop letting her get in the bed though. Things came to a head when I caught chicken pox and Mum phoned the doctor. If I had known he was coming I would have been prepared. When he came in, Puppy scrambled up to the top of the bed, poked her head over the top of the sheet, had a good look at him and then wriggled back the way she had come. Then when the doctor came across to the bed and pulled my jacket open so that he could look at my spots, the white mouse that I used to carry round everywhere with me, until I lost it in the school library, popped out of my pyjama pocket. The doctor was a bit rude to Mum about that but she had not known either the dog or the mouse was there.

Now, with the fox cubs in the bathroom, we saw yet another side to Puppy's character. She was trying frantically to get into the bathroom. Mum was cross because she had been scratching so determinedly at the door that she had scratched the paint off. Dad made her go back into the sitting-room but when she thought nobody was looking at her she slunk back to the bathroom and tried to scratch the door open again.

Susie, the spaniel, was just as anxious to get into the bathroom as the whippet, but in a different kind of way. She was fat and solid and comfortable and showed none of the sporting traits that you normally associate with her breed. She

15.

had one passion in life, food. She would go round the room after we had had a meal and lick up every single crumb she could find. Even then she would go round another couple of times in case she had overlooked anything. Dad reckoned she was only half dog, the other half was carpet sweeper. She would sample anything. She ate a whole battalion of plastic soldiers once, and once when Mum put her dinner in a plastic bowl, she ate the bowl as well.

We had collected Susie from the RSPCA animal shelter at Portsmouth, leastways we never did decide if we collected Susie or if she collected us.

We had gone down to collect some gulls that had been caught in an oil slick, and the man had said, 'I've got a spaniel here that's looking for a home. It'll make a nice dog if it has a bit of attention. The people who brought it in said they're going abroad but they all say that, it's just an excuse to get rid of them. I expect they got tired of it the same as all the others, found out it cost a bit more to keep

than they had thought or that it needed more exercise than they wanted themselves.'

He opened the door of the run so that we could look at her. The dog stood up lazily, stretched and walked right out of the door and out to our car. The back door was still open, so she climbed in and settled down. We had a spaniel.

She had been a bit difficult at first. If we went near her when she had food, she would growl and show her teeth, and if Mum got the broom out to sweep the floor, Susie would cower back against the wall, snapping and growling. Mum thought that somebody must have hit her to make her behave like that. It took her a long time to get over that, but eventually she came round and became as sloppy as only spaniels can.

She was very possessive about all four of us. She stuck to us like glue and we began to feel guilty if we went out without her. Sometimes she became a bit too possessive. If we went out in the car and stopped to go into a shop or

something, she would sit and howl until we came out again. It was dreadful.

One day Mum had taken her to school with her. She had jumped into the car when Mum went out and Mum did not have the heart to turn her out. Mum said she was all right until the children started singing in assembly. She joined in. When everybody else stopped, Susie simply carried on. Mum said it was embarrassing. The head tried to read the lesson and say the prayer as if nothing was happening, but it was a bit difficult, and most of the children were giggling anyway. In the end Mum had to go and get Susie out of the car, and she ambled round behind her for the rest of the day as good as gold.

We thought Susie must have had pups before she came to us. Perhaps the memory of her own young aroused her maternal instinct when she heard those fox cubs cry, for she became desperate to get into the bathroom. We kept her well away though because we did not know how she would behave when she saw them. We did not think she would be nasty, but we did not know and we were not going to risk it.

Those cubs did have one interesting effect on her though. She lost her gluelike attachment to us and transferred it to the bathroom door. From then on she lay outside that door, attracted to it like a magnet. We became so used to stepping over her when we wanted to go along to the bathroom that we often forgot she was there.

chapter three

It took a bit of time to get the fox cubs to start feeding, but once they got the idea they were no trouble at all. We fed them on ordinary cow's milk, using half milk and half boiled water, and we added things like glucose, calcium and extra vitamins. They swallowed the mixture easily enough once we got it into their throats, but the problem was getting it there in the first place. Mum had got the bottle out that we had used when we reared June, the little roe deer we had had the previous summer. That did amuse Sophie. The bottle was bigger than any of the cubs. There was no hope of getting the teat inside their mouths, it was much too big.

Then Sophie thought of her doll's bottle and ran to get it. It was the right size, but the hole at the top was barely more than a pinprick and it was a real problem getting the liquid through it. Dad tried, but he got more down his arm and shirt than he got into the bottle. Mum tried. She did not do much better but she did manage to get the small bottle half-full. When she eased the plastic teat into the mouth of the largest cub, he shook his head weakly from side to side and the liquid dribbled down his fur. I do not think he swallowed any of it. Even Mum did not have the patience to try to fill that bottle again, so she fetched the fountain pen filler that we were using for a leveret we were rearing. It was an ordinary filler, but we had fastened a length of valve rubber over the glass end so that it did not feel so uncomfortable in the animal's mouth.

That was easier altogether. The cub did not like having the tube pushed to the back of his mouth, but at least he took the food. He did not have any choice really, because once the tube was in place at the back of his throat, we squeezed the rubber bulb at the end of the tube and the milk squirted down his throat and he swallowed involuntarily.

We gave the cubs three fillers-full each. It was difficult to know how much they needed, but we knew there was a risk of overfeeding them, especially as they had been some time without food. Three seemed to satisfy them, and they settled back on the hay in their basket with contented little grunts.

Sophie and I were amazed at the size of their mouths, which were enormous for such tiny animals. It was when we eased them open so that we could push the valve rubber inside that we realized exactly how big they were. They were so large that they seemed to split their masks in two, and they stretched almost as far back as their ears. Their tongues too were much larger than we had expected. In fact their whole heads were large in comparison with the rest of their bodies and seemed quite out of proportion.

The cubs soon became used to the fountain pen fillers and the feeding times. We fed them every three hours, and they could tell the time as regularly as clockwork. As feeding time approached they grew restive and their crying became more and more persistent and penetrating. As soon as they started to suck the milk, they would quieten. After three fillers-full each, they would settle back into the warmth of their basket. Besides the heat of the bathroom heater, Mum would give them a hot-water bottle as well and wrap it up in some furry material she had. The three of them loved this and would snuggle against it.

At first they thought we were going to feed them every time we opened the lid of their basket, which was pretty often because Sophie was always bringing friends home from school who wanted to see the trio. Lots of my friends wanted to see them as well. I wonder why foxes have the effect they do on people. We are always having animals and birds in of one sort or another and some of them are really fascinating, but as soon as I mentioned that we had some fox cubs at home, well, all my friends wanted to come up and see them. It was not that they only wanted to see them, they liked to stroke them and touch them and pick them up.

The cubs soon settled down to regular feeding. Within five days all of them seemed to have accepted the three-hourly feeds. The thing that worried Mum was the fact that they were getting more and more potbellied and there was not a sign of any of them making a mess. We added some extra sugar to their diet and gave them some liquid paraffin, but this did not have any effect at all. We had had this trouble with other young animals, especially leverets. If they become too constipated, it causes problems, and if you use medicine to sort it out you can start exactly the other effect and they get diarrhoea. Mum said she was going to take the cubs to the vet's the next day if they still had not made a mess, but the whole thing sorted itself out.

Sophie was getting ready for bed and went along to the bathroom to clean her teeth when she let out a great wail. 'Quick,' she shouted, 'Susie's in with the cubs.'

I have never seen Mum move so quickly in her life. She had been cutting out a dress for Sophie. She gets these enthusiasms from time to time and needlework is one that keeps turning up. Luckily I do not have to wear the results and she never has the audacity to wear anything that she has made herself. It is Sophie that has the collection of homemade clothes, some of which are rather peculiarly shaped. Anyway, the lot went flying that night and Mum dashed along to the bathroom leaving a trail of thread and pins and material.

Susie had not only pushed her way into the bathroom, she had pushed the lid of the basket up as well. She was nosing those cubs violently, turning them over and over as if they were discarded toys. The three cubs had been pushed to three different corners of the basket and they were trying to whimper their protests, but each sound they made was strangled in their throats as Susie tumbled them over again. I was going to pull her off but Mum stopped me.

'Can't you see what she's doing?' she asked. 'She's cleaning them up the same as their own mother would. She's not hurting them.'

That was just what she was doing. She licked them with her big red tongue where the milk had spilled down their chests when they had been fed, then she upended them and gave their rear ends the same treatment. Then, for good measure, she gave each of them a big wet, prolonged lick that seemed to encompass all of them.

She seemed to us to be much rougher on them than was necessary, but at least her actions had one desired effect. A neat mess was deposited in each of three corners. Mum explained to Sophie that this was how the vixen would have cleaned them in the wild, that by licking their stomachs and their rear ends, the vixen not only kept the young animals clean but ensured that food passed through them and they did not become constipated. Susie had only been treating them as their own mother would have done.

We did not bother too much about Susie being with the cubs after that. We just had to make sure that she was not too attentive, for nobody could have accused Susie of being half-hearted in the attention she gave them. After they had had their meal, all they seemed to want to do was snuggle down into a little heap and go to sleep. That was not Susie's idea. That was when she decided they needed the most violent washing session of all. We could not decide if it was the smell of food or a trickle of milk on their fur which she could taste that made her choose this time, or perhaps her maternal instinct was at its strongest at feeding time. Whatever the reason, she would nose them and push them and lick them until they were scattered in different parts of the basket, crying out in temper as they tried to resettle themselves against the hot-water bottle.

We used to shut the spaniel outside the bathroom then so the cubs could have some peace, and she would immediately resume her life as a slip mat, nose pressed firmly against the gap at the bottom of the door and sighing from time to time a great reverberating sound that let us know she was becoming very, very tired of waiting. It was quite disconcerting having a bath with Susie's noisy, impatient sighs breaking the silence. As soon as we opened the door, she was in like a bulldozer, forcing the lid of the basket up and nosing those poor recumbent cubs into instant wakefulness. When she did let them relax, which was not very often, she would lie down beside the basket, gathering the bathroom mats into an untidy pile, and it was only the smell of food that would tempt her away.

Although Susie's interest was purely maternal, Puppy's was anything but. She growled when she first saw the cubs, and I think she would have snapped at them had she had the chance, but I pulled her away and shut her outside. We

were very careful after that to make sure that the whippet was kept out each time we allowed Susie to go in with the young foxes.

Sophie was the one that kept on forgetting. She never could remember if she had shut the door or not and would have to go back and check. 'Door' became a catchword in our house. Every time we saw Sophie coming from the direction of the bathroom we would shout, 'Door.' Nine times out of ten she would say, 'Oh dear,' and rush back the way she had come.

chapter four

Now that Susie had decided to take a hand in rearing the cubs, an organized routine and three-hourly feeds went by the board. She was in with those young animals at all hours of the day, and every time she roused them, the cubs thought it was time for another feed and set up such a chorus of crying.

They had changed a lot in those first couple of weeks and were really beginning to look like little foxes. Their heads were still rounded and their soft fur was still the same chocolate brown colour, but their eyes, which were soft and gentle and observant, had turned brown. All of them had had runny and watery eyes in those first few days, but Dad had bathed them with some special eye lotion he had and they had cleared up beautifully. Their ears, too, were erect now although they were still rounded in shape. They had seemed just like puppies' ears at first until I saw how carefully they had been folded, just like you fold an envelope. I suppose it was nature's way of protecting the eardrums during birth.

Their feeding habits were changing almost daily now. It had not taken any of them long to recognize the fountain pen filler, nor did they need much encouragement to start sucking when we eased it into their mouths. The largest of the three sucked so violently and started to take so much with each swallow that I found it difficult to refill it quickly enough. He would be clambering up me trying to get at the filler before I was ready for him. So one day, when I had already given him eight fillers-full and he still wanted more, I thrust the dish beneath his nose and told him to get on with it. He did too. He lapped enthusiastically and tipped the bowl right over and I was covered in the sticky stuff; so was he, but Susie soon dealt with him in her over-enthusiastic manner.

If he could lap so could the other two, I thought, but they were not as forward as the bigger dog fox and they needed a bit of coaxing. I dipped the spoon into the warm liquid and kept wetting their muzzles so that they got the idea in the end and started to lap. It took a bit of time and patience, particularly with the smallest of the trio. We were adding baby foods to the milk now and cereals and all sorts of things that we thought would do young animals good. They were prepared to try anything, especially that dog fox.

The dog was the largest of the three, and he seemed more advanced and more adventuresome than the others from the beginning. He would immediately have his nose in any food we put out for them. The other two approached food much more cautiously, and the quietest one of the three often had to be coaxed to try it at all. This is where Susie was so good. Normally she was uncontrollable if there was even the smell of food about, but now she would sit back and watch those cubs eat with a real matronly air. Mind you, she would lick the plate clean for them if they left the slightest trace on it or even if they were not getting on with their meal quickly enough. She would get a bit impatient too if she thought they were eating too much and in the end she would push her head between them and completely clear the dish, turning it upside down and giving the bottom of it a few licks for good measure.

Mum nearly had a fit once when she saw Sophie take the plate from which the foxes had been feeding and put it back on the kitchen shelf.

'Well, Susie's got it as clean as we do when we do the washing up,' Sophie argued.

The three cubs were really growing into lovely little animals, soft and brown and attractive. Every time I went in to see how they were I wasted an hour or more just looking at them or stroking them. Sophie was worse than me. She would have had them out with her dolls and given them rides in her baby carriage if Mum had let her. They were just the sort of animals you wanted to pick up and fondle. I used to sit for ages with them on my lap. Although the two larger ones tolerated being handled they did not really enjoy it, and after a time they would grow restless and irritable and would wriggle and scrabble their way on to the floor. But the smallest one would sit for ages while I stroked her. When I rubbed her between the ears or eyes she squirmed and shut her eyes.

We called this smallest one Jenny. It seemed to suit her, for she was so much softer than the other two. Sophie was always thinking of names for the cubs, often changing them two or three times a day, but Jenny was the first she suggested for this smallest one and we never changed it.

We were having our meal one evening when there was this dreadful noise from the bathroom. It sounded as if something had been hurt badly, and the suddenness of it startled us all for a second. We sat staring at each other, our knives and forks poised in our hands, wondering what was happening. Then I was up and running to that room.

It was the dog fox. He had found his way out of the basket and he could not get back. He was sitting there, in the middle of the rug, with his head back and his nose pointing towards the ceiling, howling in the most discordant way. I had never heard a noise like it. It sounded a bit like a spoiled child who has been told for the first time that he cannot have something he has demanded, and a bit like a peacock in love.

He looked so funny that I had to go and get the others to come to have a look at him. Mum reckoned Susie must have opened the basket for him to get out, because the lid was much too heavy for such a small animal to push it up by himself. We persuaded Susie to come back into the dining-room, but she was most reluctant to leave the bathroom until she smelled the food that was still on the table. Ten minutes later the same unmusical noise started up again. There was the fox cub sitting in the middle of the bathroom rug once more. Obviously he did not need any assistance to get out.

The next day all three of the young animals were out and walking round the floor. It would not have been so bad if they had not been such messy little creatures. I often wondered why Mum had been so anxious for them to make a mess when we first had them. Now they never seemed to stop. Not only did I have to get the cubs back into the basket, I had to get busy with the disinfectant. I did not like the job very much.

We weighted the lid of the basket down, but that only proved a temporary measure, for within a couple of days those cubs were out again. We made leather straps to tie round the basket and keep it firmly closed, but they soon wormed their way out. There must have been a two-inch gap at the most, but it was enough for the three of them to squirm their way out, although we could never see how they could do it.

For the first few days the exertions of getting out seemed to tire them, and they seemed content to sit on the rug or stand there with their bodies close to the ground and their overlarge heads drooping. Then they started shambling about, stopping frequently for rests. Little Jenny was always the quietest. She would follow the others about for a bit and then simply give up and sit down. The other two moved ceaselessly once they were out of the basket, only pausing to look at a fly or one of the dogs or anything else they considered interesting.

When something caught their attention they would really study it, cocking their heads first this side, then the other, moving right around it so that they could watch it from a different direction. Sometimes they would turn their heads right around so that they were looking at something upside down. Sometimes they turned their heads just a little too far so that they tipped right over and tumbled head over heels right on top of the thing they were trying to watch.

chapter five

All at once they were not baby animals any longer. They were young foxes. We did not see them change. Handling them each day as we did we had not noticed how they were developing. One day I went in to feed the three of them, but Susie had beaten me to it as she so often did and forced the lid of the basket up. The trio of cubs sat there, waiting and watching me expectantly. As they saw the dish in my hand, they scrabbled up the side. That was when I realized they had grown into tiny foxes, complete miniatures of the beautiful animals they were to become.

Their faces had lengthened and grown more pointed, although their mouths still seemed exceptionally large. Their sharp little noses were forever twitching. Their floppy brown ears had become the fox's characteristic pointed ones. Their fur was still the same chocolate brown colour, but already a thin ginger line was showing itself along the spines of the two larger animals.

They were really lively now, all three of them. A washcloth dropped on the floor was pounced on immediately, pulled back into the corner and shredded with much enthusiasm. A toothbrush proved great sport and Mum was really cross when we forgot to hang the towels up out of their reach, because the cubs would scramble up and get hold of a corner in their teeth and pull the whole thing down; there was never any chance of using any article for its original purpose once the fox cubs had had a go at it.

They really enjoyed it if they could bite into something, for their small sharp teeth were pushing through their gums now and they liked to try them out. Sophie gave them her old slippers and they tore them to bits with real enthusiasm.

The only trouble was that she left her new ones in there when she had a bath and the cubs treated them in the same way. It was a bit awkward when visitors came and used the bathroom. They did not always appreciate being attacked by three lively fox cubs when they were least expecting it.

The cubs were not supposed to be out of the basket unless we were there, but those animals were real escapists and we found it almost impossible to keep them in. If Susie did not encourage them, then they found their own way out. We would have to get them into a run outside. The trouble was that we had not weaned them from the heat and still kept the heater on for them during the night.

Things came to a climax rather suddenly.

One day, Susie not only opened the basket for the cubs, she left the bathroom door open as well. The first Mum knew anything about it was when she turned round to reach for something on the shelf and tripped over Jenny. Jenny was put back in the basket quickly enough, but there was no sign of the other two. It was not hard to trace their progress. They had deposited messes pretty regularly, but, even at that young age, they were secretive animals and were as likely to be behind something as in it.

We had everything out of cupboards and off tables. We emptied our toy boxes and took all the books from the shelves. We found the little vixen crammed behind the kitchen cabinet in a space so narrow that we could not see how she had got her head in there, let alone the rest of her. There was not a sign of the dog fox. We did not see where he could be. Mum thought he must have got outside somehow even though all the doors were shut. We did not see where else he could be.

Dad was not particularly worried when he came home. 'He'll come out all right when he's hungry,' he said.

Mum had gone out to get tea and we were looking at television when there was a crash, a startled scream and a high-pitched squeal. We were all on our feet immediately

and dashed towards the noise. There was Mum standing in the middle of the kitchen floor with all the cutlery scattered around her, declaring that her big toe would never be the same again. A very frightened fox cub was crouched in the corner of the room.

He had been in the cutlery drawer all the time. Nobody had thought of looking there. Mum had gone to get a knife from the drawer, and as she pulled it open she had seen the fox. He must have climbed up into the back of the drawer and been there all the time we had been searching. It gave Mum such a shock that she had held on to the drawer and pulled the whole thing out, on to her toes, as she kept reminding us. I think it gave the cub a shock too because he was very subdued for the whole of the next day.

The cubs were out of the basket the next day as well. They could not get out of the bathroom door because Dad had put a bolt on it so that we could make sure it was kept shut. One or two visitors seemed a little surprised that we wanted to bolt the outside of the bathroom. One business friend of Dad's who came from Norway seemed to think it was a peculiar British habit and kept saying in a puzzled voice, 'In Norway, we always lock the door on the inside when we are in there.' I do not think he ever really understood what had made the outside lock necessary.

This time the foxes had disappeared again. There was only Jenny sitting there in the basket and there was not a sign of the other two although Mum knew they must be in the room. Then she saw the gap in the linen cupboard door. The cubs had seen it first. The little vixen had only managed to clamber up to the first shelf, but the dog had clambered right up to the top. You can imagine the mess. Mum was washing sheets and towels long after we had gone to bed.

The day after that, Mum was reading a magazine and found an article about how young animals can transfer diseases to small children and how some of those diseases can lie dormant for years on end. The article mentioned a form of blindness which affected some people and could be traced back to the fact that they had played with kittens or other young animals when they were children.

That really worried Mum. She phoned the vet straight away, and Sophie and I could hear her talking to him. 'Well, what are the chances of the children picking up something from them . . . ?

'I don't care how remote the possibility is. Is there a chance at all that the children can pick up something from them . . . ?

'They're playing with them all the time . . .

'Of course they're careful about washing their hands. I know that foxes are more likely to carry disease than domestic animals . . .

'One chance in ten thousand you reckon. Well, it strikes me the sooner we get them outside the better.'

Mum was really fussy after that. She kept making Sophie and me wash our hands in disinfectant even when we had not been near the cubs. It seemed daft that we had to wash when we came out of the bathroom rather than when we went in it. We had to have a bath every night as well, and she even put disinfectant in the bath. I thought that was going a bit too far but she insisted. You can guess what we both began to smell like and what my friends said. I reckon we must have been the healthiest-smelling family in the area.

Sophie did not like the smell of disinfectant. I did not either but I did not go on about it. In the end she took a bottle of lavender water and poured that everywhere that Mum had put the disinfectant. Phew. You should have smelled it, lavender and disinfectant mixed together. It was dreadful. What was more, we could not get rid of it and the bathroom stank for days.

Mum gets these bees in her bonnet about different things from time to time. Dad used to tease her about them, which generally made her more earnest about them than ever. Germs was one of the things that she went on about. She would go weeks without any mention of them, and then she would start about the health dangers you face when you deal with wild animals. Every day she would scrub down everything in sight. We always did use a gallon of disinfectant a month, but we had to double the order when she had a germ campaign under way. Dad would ask if she had taken out shares in a disinfectant plant or if she was wearing a new perfume. When she started up about the cubs and the transferring of disease and infection, I was surprised to find that Dad was just as serious as she was.

'Yes, I've been thinking about that,' he said. 'It's not too bad while they're tiny, but even then it's not hygienic to have them in the house, not that we've really had much choice. Now that we can't keep them in the basket they must go outside as soon as possible.'

He started on their run that night, and Sophie and I could hear him banging away long after we had gone to bed. He had run the car round to the paddock so that he could use the car headlights for light. We still had the sections of an otter run. We had only dismantled it a few weeks before. Dad was reassembling it and making sure that there were not any holes left through which the cubs could get out.

It took him two nights to complete. He left me to put the small animals out there before I went to school. He had meant to give me a hand, but when it was time for him to get the car out so that he would be ready for work, he found that he had used the headlights a bit too long the night before and the battery was as flat as a pancake. The starter whined weakly the first couple of times he pulled it and then died out altogether. So Sophie and I had to help him push the car out. Even then it did not want to go and if the farmer had not come along with his tractor and given us a hand it would probably be there still.

Of course that made Dad late and he went off in his usual rush.

There was nobody like Dad for liking to start his day in a well-organized way, with everything worked out almost like a ritual. He allowed himself so much time for getting washed and dressed in the morning and so long to spend with his birds. He spent the same time over his breakfast each day. At least that was the idea, only it never worked out that way. Generally something unexpected happened.

Once he woke up and found the old pony had her head jammed through the bedroom window and was gazing at him unconcernedly. We had to get her back into the paddock, find the way she had got out and patch up the hole before we did anything else that morning. Then there was the time the pony followed him into the house, through the front door. We had one of those long, narrow passages in the centre of the cottage and Peggy Pony was pretty round, as round as the passage was narrow in fact. We had a real job pushing her backwards to get her out again. There always seemed to be something happening, and I do not think I can ever remember a time Dad made the well-organized departure he had planned.

Anyway, it was the car that day, and Sophie said she would give me a hand getting the cubs across to the run. Those young foxes seemed to know they were going outside and they really played up. Jenny was all right and she snuggled contentedly into my arms when I picked her up, but the other two were out of the basket as soon as I opened the lid and into the linen cupboard. Every time I lunged at one of them it seemed to wriggle out of the way behind some towels or sheets or something and elude my grasp. That dog fox had made a mess the minute he had got in the cupboard, and when I reached out to get him, I put my hand right in it. That made Sophie giggle, and once she starts laughing she is not much use for anything.

We caught them all in the end. I gave Sophie the dog fox to carry and I managed the other two. We were half-way across to the paddock, where Dad had put the run, when there was a yell from Sophie, 'Oh! He just jumped out of my arms,' she cried.

I shut the two young vixens in the run quickly and ran back to give Sophie a hand with the dog, but he had disap-peared in that short time. She had not seen where he had gone and the two of us were crawling up and down on our hands and knees looking in the thick laurel bushes for him. I know it was not really Sophie's fault. That dog fox was a muscular little animal, and he had suddenly pushed him-self against her body, levering himself upwards, then he had twisted and jumped before she had had a chance to realize what was happening. All the same I was cross with her.

Then Mum was shouting that Sophie would miss the bus. No one seemed to mind if I missed it, which I did fre-quently. I way always having to get my bike out and try to race the bus to Grantham. This was not such a difficult thing to do because the bus travels all round the villages picking up the other children.

Mum saw Sophie off and then came across and gave me a hand searching. She was in a hurry herself because she had to get to school. She laddered her tights, crawling along the hedge, which did not improve her temper, but there was no sign of the cub. I reached the end of the hedge and sat down to look back the way I had come and there, sitting on the grass watching our progress with ob-vious interest, was Susie. Sitting beside Susie, with his head cocked a little to one side, looking at us as if he was won-dering whatever we were up to, was the young dog fox. I do not know how long he had been there. I did not spend any time wondering either. I picked him up quickly, stowed him in the run with the others and hurried back to the cottage. As I reached the gate, I looked back. All three cubs were sitting in a row looking at me, heads cocked a little to one side. I felt guilty at leaving them.

chapter six

I was really late for school that day. Not only had the school bus been and gone, but the boys were just coming out of assembly. The other boys used to laugh when I had to explain why I was late. It would have been so much easier to have said we had overslept or the alarm clock had not gone off or something like that, but Dad used to insist that we tell the truth because it always paid in the end. All the boys were standing round with grins on their faces. I suppose they must have guessed by the way I was puffing that something unusual had happened. I think most of the teachers used to think I made up my excuses. I am sure the deputy head did, because as soon as he saw that I was late, he would put up his hand and say, 'All right, all right, Burkett. I'll believe you. You've been chasing a chimpanzee up the chimney.'

The headmaster was pretty understanding though. He knew how busy we could get from time to time and he never used to grumble. He seemed to appreciate that sometimes I had to help Mum and Dad. Even so, it sounded a bit lame standing in the hall and saying, 'Mum and I had to chase a fox up the laurel hedge, sir.'

He bent his head forward and looked at me over the top of his glasses. 'Did you catch it, Burkett? That's the important thing. Always catch your fox.'

'Oh yes, thank you, sir.'

The other boys always asked the same question. 'Is it true? Did you really have to chase a fox?'

I was lucky I had got off so lightly, especially as I had already been late earlier on in the week. I had been so late then that I had completely missed the first lesson. I think the headmaster would have been cross about that, but my explanation really took the wind out of his sails.

'I had to help Mum rescue Mrs Nicholson from a swan, sir.'

I suppose it did sound a bit daft in the calm of a well-ordered school, but at home it had been a real emergency. The postman had come dashing into the house quite out of breath. Would Mum go up to the village quickly? The swan that had been on the pond out across the meadow had suddenly turned nasty. When Mrs Nicholson had gone out to hang up her wash, the swan had appeared round the corner of the house. It had spread its wings and gone for her. She had dropped everything and run into the garden shed and shut the door. The swan had gone as well and was attacking the shed door trying to get in to her. It was lucky the postman had a letter for her and heard her shouting, because the neighbours on both sides were out at work and I do not know how long she would have had to stay there.

It happened to be one of those days when everything had run along its ordered lines like clockwork and I was down at the corner waiting for the bus. In fact it was coming over the hill when Mum called out for me to come back in a hurry.

Mrs Nicholson's garden was exactly as the postman had described it. She was in the shed and she refused even to unlock the door, let alone open it. It was small wonder, for the swan was reared right up to its full height, and it was tall enough to look me straight in the eye. With its outspread wings it looked really formidable. Across the lawn, torn and dirty pieces of linen were scattered. Obviously the bird had been throwing them about.

Mum was used to handling swans, but she needed my help with this one because it was so large. She folded its wings into its body and tucked the whole parcel under her arm. 'The poor thing's starving,' Mum told the lady in the shed, but I do not think Mrs Nicholson was concerned about

the swan. She was more worried about her wash. I held the
bird firmly on the back seat while Mum drove home. We
put it in a shed with a bucketful of food before we both
dashed off to our respective schools.

It was not an unusual story. Many people feed swans in
the summer months but do not spare them a thought in
the winter when their natural food supply is short. Sometimes the birds have become so used to taking food from
visitors they will not forage for themselves. This one had
turned nasty simply because it was so hungry.

We fed it up, then clipped a wing and took it to a lake
about twenty miles away where a lady promised to feed it
each day for us. It is still there now.

I suppose the excuse about the fox seemed quite mild
after the one about the swan. Anyway, the headmaster
seemed to accept it without a qualm.

When we got home, Sophie and I went right out to see
how the cubs were. They were sitting there in a line, as

still as statues. They were in exactly the same places in which they had been when I left them, or so it seemed. All three of them stared expectantly towards us. We had them out straight away and they seemed really pleased to see us.

Jenny just sat on Sophie's lap and the other little vixen semed quite happy lying on the grass beside us, her pointed head, which seemed out of all proportion to her little body, resting on her forepaws while she looked around. The young dog was a bit more adventuresome and would run a few feet away from us. If there was any noise such as from an aeroplane flying overhead or a car going up the road, then he would be back sitting near us immediately, looking expectantly in the direction of the sound that had disturbed him.

It amused Sophie to see the way those three animals acted when they heard a new sound. Their first reaction was to sit down. They would sit down so quickly and so exactly at the same moment that it used to make her giggle. At the same time the cubs would look in the direction from which the sound had come. The first time a motorbike went up the lane alongside the paddock, the foxes went through this routine. We could see them following the noise as it receded up the hill towards the farm, but they did not move their heads. They moved their ears. We watched as their ears turned with the direction of the bike's sound.

Once their ears had unfolded, they had quickly lost their rounded appearance and developed the characteristic pointed look. They always seemed large for the size of the animal; 'butterfly ears,' Dad used to call them. As soon as the ears had grown like this, the cubs had immediately developed the ability to move each ear independently of the other one. We would often sit and watch them as they moved one ear round to catch a sound on their right side while the other ear was twisted towards a completely different sound. After the noise had gone, they would sit there immobile for a few more seconds, then, giving little shakes, they would resume their wandering until something else disturbed them.

Their hearing was really acute. Sometimes the three of them would freeze and look in the same direction. We knew by the way they moved their ears that they had picked up some sound, but it would be several seconds later before we heard it too – perhaps a truck winding down the hill from the village or somebody using a saw up in the woods. Whatever the noise, those cubs always seemed to hear it before we did.

Their eyes were keen as well. Even at this age, they would suddenly leap into the long grass, and we would find they had jumped at a small insect or a butterfly which was so well camouflaged against the background of the hedge or the grass that we had to get really close before we could see it.

Their sense of smell developed early too. As soon as Mum started to cook their meat, you could see their noses twitching, and they would sit and stare expectantly in the direction of the cottage. We always gave them cooked food. Mum thought it might dull their killing instinct. They might more easily associate raw meat with the animals from which it came.

Sometimes one of them would sit down, and I could see its nose twitching. I would watch it as it went forward, its nose moving the whole time. Then it would scrabble in the undergrowth and retrieve a candy wrapper, or something like that, which looked as though it had been there for ages. It must have retained some kind of smell, however, because the cub would nose it around, and even chew the whole thing up on some occasions.

chapter seven

The cubs soon accepted their new routine. I would go out first thing in the morning to feed them. At first I used to let them out for a run as well, but as they grew bigger they seemed to be more reluctant to go back when it was time for me to go and get ready for school, especially that young dog. Once or twice he ran round the other side of the run when he saw me going to get him and sat there looking at me. He turned and went the other way when I went round after him. The two of us would be facing each other on opposite sides of the run. When I took a few steps to the right, so did he. If I went to the left, he did the same. If Sophie was about, it was all right. She would come and give me a hand catching him. As soon as he saw her coming, that fox knew he had lost and he would trot into the run completely unconcerned.

One day though, Sophie did not hear me calling and went off to school. It took me the best part of half an hour to catch that cub that morning. He had me running round and round the run after him. When I did catch him, he looked up at me with such an angelic look on his face that I could have crowned him. At school that day I said I had had a puncture. I know I should not have done, but I could not very well say that I had spent all that time running round a pen after a fox cub.

When I left each morning and looked back at the run, all three cubs would be sitting there in a row, small heads tipped a little to one side, watching me intently. I could almost imagine them saying, 'Can't we come too?' I hated leaving them.

They would be in the same position when we got home

in the evening, and if Mum had not told us differently we would have thought that they had stayed there all day long. They never needed a second invitation to come out. As soon as we went towards the run, Susie would appear and come out with us. Mum said she spent most of the day just lying alongside the run and only the smell of food would tempt her away. Now, as the cubs came out, she would wash each one of them in turn, licking them so fiercely that they would tumble head over heels. They did not seem to mind as much as they had done when they had been tiny. Sometimes the young dog would grunt and grumble as if he did not hold with all that cleanliness, and the larger of the two vixens would become a bit restive, but Jenny never complained. She must have been the cleanest fox cub in the whole world.

They were growing really playful now. They would run up and down on the patch of grass outside their pen; in fact they began to wear the grass away altogether. Their gait was awkward and ungainly, for their feet were soft and big and out of proportion to the rest of their bodies. Sometimes they looked like little puppies, except when they walked, for then they moved with the stealth of a cat, putting one foot immediately in front of the other so that all of their four feet seemed to travel in a single straight line.

Even in their play you could see the way they were developing as young foxes. They would stalk low along the ground, then freeze suddenly and hold that position for seconds at a time. They would creep through the long grass and then, abandoning all attempts at concealment, would leap out like miniature rockets. Then they would really play with the exuberance of young things, bounding round and round, up and down, until they sank down on the ground completely exhausted with their large tongues lolling out of their equally large mouths.

They were aware of and interested in everything that

moved. A beetle ambling across the path would really arouse their curiosity and they would follow it along, their noses getting nearer and nearer the ground until they were all but pressed right into the poor insect.

I shall never forget the time the young dog fox came running back along the path and met a buttercup nodding gently in the breeze. He stopped and looked. Then he put one paw up hesitatingly and dabbed at it. Immediately the yellow head of the flower sprang back, waving violently, and the cub sat down in surprise. He repeated his investigation, and again the flower sprang back. This time the cub sat right up on his hind legs and knocked it with both paws, one after the other, missing it completely and tipping backwards into a furry ball. He sat back and looked at the flower with suspicion. Then he sidled by, keeping as far away from the buttercup as possible while remaining on the path, and ran all the way back to us. The cubs seemed to have a very strong homing instinct. We were relieved to see this.

There was always something aloof about the two largest cubs. They never liked being fussed over and handled as Jenny did. When we picked them up, they would tolerate it for a short while and then push against our bodies in their efforts to get down. At first they ranged only a few feet away from the run, but soon they were going forty to fifty feet away and the only way we could know where they were was by watching out for the movement of the long grass. Peggy Pony never did do the grass justice, and the field generally resembled a miniature jungle more than anything else.

Peggy Pony was not much help with our efforts to tame the cubs either. She seemed to think something was going on and she was being left out. She would amble over and push herself right in between Sophie and me. Then she would bend right down and nose the little animals. The trouble was that instead of sniffing she would generally blow through her nostrils. The first time she did that the cubs wondered what was happening and scurried back into their run, except for the dog. He sat up and looked at her as if he could not believe his eyes. When she did it again he fell over backwards and I could almost see the look of surprise on his face. Peggy Pony was still not satisfied.

Not only did she get between Sophie and me, but, with great sighs and various other horsy noises, she would settle herself down until she was lying between us. Then, rolling right over on to her back, she would hold her four legs stiffly skyward and we would have to rub her tummy. I did anyway; Sophie used to say it made her fingernails dirty. Peggy Pony was almost forty then and a bit rheumatic, so Sophie and I would often have to give her a good helping shove when she rolled back and tried to regain her feet.

The cubs were a bit worried about her great bulk at first, but they soon learned to accept her and would run round her hoofs quite happily. The pony learned to accept them too and would spend most of the day standing near their run, wandering over to have a good look at them every so often.

We started taking the cubs for little walks round the field, teaching them to walk to heel. It would have been a little easier if Peggy had not insisted on coming too. I would walk along one of the well-worn paths that the pony had made, with Susie stuck hard to my heel and the three little cubs in line behind her. Peggy Pony lumbered along behind them at the end of the queue. Those little cubs were so good. Sometimes they would wander off a bit, but they would always resume their place in the line before we were back at their pen.

Mum would have their food ready then and they knew it. We wanted them to get used to regular feeding habits and times and to appreciate that the food would be there when they came back from their walk. That way they had something to come back for.

Feeding was the least of the worries. They were prepared to try anything, and they would go crazy if they smelled chocolate. Sometimes Sophie would have a chocolate wrapper in her pocket and could not understand why all three cubs were scrabbling up her legs. As soon as she had felt in her pocket and thrown out the paper, they lost interest in her.

At feeding times they would pick out the bits of food they liked best and tug them away to their different corners. Even at this young age, they tried to keep the food to themselves. Once Dad tried to get them used to having food taken away from them, like you train a dog. He had only bent down to lift the plate when one of the foxes seized his hand, really fastening its teeth into him and drawing blood. If one of the others approached a cub while it was eating, it would snarl and show its teeth. Even Jenny was the same. It was not that they were short of food. We gave them plenty, more than they could eat. They were just as nasty with the surplus food and would tug it with the same possessiveness to bury it in a corner or beneath their bedding.

chapter eight

At four and a half months old those cubs were delightful.
Their chocolate brown fur was giving way to a ginger coat,
so they looked a little moth-eaten. Otherwise they were the
picture of health, alert, active and fit. It was at this stage
Sophie announced that she had finally decided on their
names. They were to be called Tom, Fred and Jenny. The
dog fox was Tom, the quiet little vixen was Jenny and the
other one was Fred.

'You can't call them Tom, Fred and Jenny,' I told her.
'Only one of them's a boy.'

'I don't care,' she said. 'They look like Tom, Fred and
Jenny, so that's what I'm going to call them.'

That is what we all came to call them in fact.

They were really playful. When we let them out in the
evenings they would dash round and round their pen, leaping over anything that was in their way, generally one of
the other cubs. Sometimes they would dash round in ever
tightening circles in front of the run, always choosing the
same spot so that the grass wore away there. Sometimes,
when one of the cubs was running at full tilt, it would stop
dead and freeze, remaining like that for a few seconds before
it started dashing madly round again. Their enthusiasm was
so infectious that I often stood and laughed at them. As for
Sophie, she would run up and down and round and round
as if she were a cub herself.

It was about this time that I found out the real disadvan-
tage of having the cubs – visitors. I had often heard Mum
and Dad say to somebody who had called unexpectedly, 'I
wish you'd let us know you were coming.'

It was not that they minded showing people what they

were trying to do, but there was so much that could be done only when they were alone with an individual animal or bird and had time to spend with it. Once a broken wing had mended, Dad would spend hours sometimes coaxing a bird to fly a short distance again. If they were disturbed when he was just getting the bird to feel its wings once more, then weeks of work would have been ruined in a matter of seconds. Sometimes it would be getting dark before people went and we would have to do the feeding by flashlight.

The fox cubs brought matters to a head. Chris, one of my school pals, was at my house, and his dad, who happened to be a reporter on the local paper, came to fetch him. Of course we showed him the fox cubs and he took some photos of them. That next week, a photo appeared in the local paper. I was ever so pleased, especially as he gave me some copies for myself. I never thought it might cause problems.

Then the first lady arrived. She was talking to Mum when I got home from school. It seemed that she had seen the photo of the cubs in the paper and had come up to see them. While she was there, she wanted to see the birds as well. The next day she came back and brought some children with her, and several other people turned up as well. By the time the light began to fade, I realized that I had not had the cubs out of the run at all, except to show them briefly to one visitor or another, and that I had not done any of the things that I had wanted to do, not even my homework.

It was the same the next day. When it started all over again the next morning, Dad put his foot down.

Sunday was always an awkward day. Often men would call round in the morning and leave their children with Mum while they talked to Dad. It happened that Sunday. We were just beginning to get the year's fledglings in, Mum was trying to feed them and keep an eye on three children who kept trying to pick them up whenever she turned her back. She wanted me to go in and give her a hand and look after these children so that she could get on with the dinner, but some other people called to see the foxes and I had to take them across the paddock. By lunchtime, we had had twenty-seven different groups of visitors, all asking the same questions. We were worn out.

When another group arrived before we had had our first course, Dad really lost his temper and shouted at them that if they had had the manners to phone up and tell us that they were coming, they would have been welcome, but he was not having anyone else walking round the garden. We felt awkward about that for a long time because it turned out that one of these visitors was one who was genuinely interested in the work we do with the animals and had come from the other side of the country to see us. The only reason that he had not phoned first was because he was not sure where we lived.

That next week, Dad strengthened the fencing and bought some strong padlocks for the gates. When the weekend came, we padlocked ourselves in, refusing to show anybody the animals unless they had phoned up and made arrangements to come. Most people understood, but some were insistent and forced their way in. One Sunday afternoon we went out and found a man had climbed the fence and set up his camera and was taking photos in the back garden. From time to time we had to call the police to get people out. Dad was quite serious when he said that if things did not improve, we would have to move, because as they were at that moment, our lives were not our own.

The number of visitors who had been calling unexpectedly had been building up for some time, but it seemed that the fox cubs had attracted even more, so that the situation had become unbearable. We avoided all publicity from then on. Mum and Dad gave up the television programmes they had been doing. They had been doing an animal programme for children once a month, and although they enjoyed it, it was another call on our privacy.

Things were much easier with the padlocks in place, and I was able to really set about training those cubs. I wanted them to come when they were called. I would let them roam off and then call them back. They soon came to recognize my voice. 'Fox, fox, fox,' I would shout.

Each time they came back I would reward them with some titbit or other, generally a piece of chicken. Occasionally I gave them chocolate, which they loved. They would quarrel over that until even the smell of it had gone. Of course Susie always reached me first, looking starved as usual, and I generally gave way and let her have a bit too. The cubs did not hesitate to join her. At first they tried to snatch and pull the titbit away, but I held it firmly and insisted that they take it gently. They soon learned. They would come up boldly enough within a few feet of me but would be hesitant about coming that last bit and actually taking the food from my fingers. I would stand still and would not move the piece of food in my hand. Gradually they would gain courage until they actually came close and stretched up and took the titbit.

Sophie used to try to help, but she would get impatient when a cub took a long time to come up to her. You could see that it really wanted to come, and several times it would reach out only to draw back at the last minute. Sophie generally lost heart first. She would shove the food towards the cub and that often frightened it away.

Sophie and I used to spend hours out in the paddock with the cubs and Susie and old Peggy Pony. Sophie was a bit of a drawback sometimes when we took them for walks, because she would insist on bringing her dolls, and they were more trouble than the cubs. Not that the cubs were really any trouble at all, they were fun. They made us laugh at the way they would tumble over each other, and how they would crouch low on the ground and growl as if they were really fierce, only to spring up like jack-in-the-boxes and dash around again with complete abandon.

Then one day they really did go too far. The wire fence between the paddock and the lawn where we kept the bigger birds of prey proved no hindrance to them and they got through it and started to play around the birds. Immediately Dad's goshawk leaned forward on its perch, tensing its talons and looking ready to pounce on the young intruders.

I shouted at the cubs. They took no notice at all. Susie sat on the grass, completely unconcerned, scratching herself nonchalantly. Now the goshawk spread its wings as Tom dabbed out at its leash. I could not get round in time. 'Susie,' I shouted.

The spaniel shook herself. Then, as if she had all the time in the world, she ambled amiably towards me. As she moved, so did the cubs. They fell in obediently behind her and followed her right across to my feet, where the four of them sat down in a line and gazed up at me, expectantly waiting for titbits.

I stood looking at the cubs. They were not tame at all. They were not coming to me when I called them. It was Susie that was coming and they were following her. When they played along the path or jumped out from the long grass, they were always near the spaniel. When I held out a titbit and called them, it was always Susie that reached me first. In the following weeks it was even more obvious. Each day they were becoming more and more adventuresome, and sometimes all three of them would disappear in different directions. They did come back if I called them but only if I called Susie first.

Things were suddenly brought to a head when Susie and the whippet decided to go off adventuring on their own. Puppy always kept her distance from those cubs. When we were out with them she was always in the vicinity and she would watch every move they made but she would never join in and would never approach them. On this particular day, Susie had been sitting near the run and the three cubs had been dashing round and round in front of her actually using her as a springboard from time to time when she got in the way. Then she suddenly seemed to lose interest and stood up, shook herself and was off across the field with Puppy dancing along at her side. The cubs stopped in their tracks and started after the dogs. As one they moved, leaping and falling, tangling with the long grass as they tried to catch up with them. I guessed what was happening immediately and called, 'Fox, fox, fox.'

They did not even slow down.

I know you are not supposed to run after animals, that you are supposed to will them to return. I did not dare risk it. I shouted to the dogs, but they were right across the next field and made no attempt to turn. I was running in the same direction.

I soon caught up with Jenny. She was sitting in the path

55

and seemed to be pleased to be picked up and taken back to the run. By the time I got back to the hedge, there was no sign of the other cubs, only the faithful old pony, who kept giving me violent nudges with her nose as if she were trying to urge me forward a bit more quickly. I clambered over the fence, ripping my trousers on the barbed wire. I would probably have been all right if the pony had not nosed me just as I was balanced on the top strand, ready to jump.

Then I was not sure where to look. Everything was so still. No grass moved. No playful cubs ran up and down the hedge. The two dogs had long ago disappeared right over the hill. Sophie came out while I was looking along the hedge and I shouted to tell her what had happened. 'Well, Susie's here,' she shouted back. 'Come on, Sue.'

Susie was ambling up the field. She must have run in a complete circle, for she was coming in from the road. As she reached Sophie, the whippet appeared too. They both looked muddy, and I remembered then that the farmer had been muck-spreading. I shouted a warning to Sophie, but I was too late. She had bent down to stroke the dogs. Only once, but it was enough. She was spattered from head to foot and her hand had turned that particular shade of khaki. Did she moan. I had to laugh, and that only made her crosser than ever. Mum came out to see what the matter was and stayed to give me a hand looking for those two cubs.

I found Fred by pure chance. As I clambered back into our paddock, I thought I saw something move in front of me. Sure enough, there was the middle-sized cub crouching down in the long grass trying to make herself small. Perhaps I was a bit eager, but as I reached out to pick her up, she snapped and caught the back of my hand with her sharp teeth. The gash was not deep but it was painful. I caught hold of her by the scruff of the neck and tapped her sharply on the nose. Then I held my fingers in front of her, daring her to bite them. She seemed to understand and drew back, burying her head in my arm.

Mum made me go and wash the cut and put some ointment on it. She said that it could become infected very easily and you must always take particular care if you are bitten by an animal.

We found Tom as well in the end, but not until we had spent two hours looking up and down and round about. Then Susie ambled up and the cub jumped out from the very spot at which we had been looking and followed her back to the run, the very picture of obedience.

chapter nine

That night we decided that we would only keep one of the cubs. 'If you want to make an animal tame you must only have one,' Dad explained. 'They retain too much of the wilder side of their nature if you keep more than one, and they always learn bad habits from each other much more easily than they learn the good ones.'

Mum phoned up two friends who had seen the cubs and fallen in love with them. They had asked if they could have one of them if we did ever decide to part with them. They came straight away although one of them had to drive more than a hundred and fifty miles to reach us. I was glad I was in bed when they arrived. I knew Mum and Dad were right and that it was much easier to keep just the one, but I liked them all.

I would have preferred to keep Tom. He was magnificent, so proud and alert and decisive. There was something arrogant about the way he moved, something confident about the way he studied his world. In his miniature way, he was true fox. Everybody else wanted to keep Jenny. She was delightful, gentle and soft, but she was not the same. She was more of a pet already. Tom was real fox.

Now that we were left with just the one, there seemed to be none of the problems we had had when there were three. We would bring Jenny over to the house as much as possible so that she would not feel lonely. She was clean. I cannot say that she never made a mess indoors, but the occasions on which she did were rare. She never ran off although she would follow Susie when she went sniffing along the hedgerows. We never had any worry about taking Jenny with us when we went out for a walk after we came home from school. Sophie and I took it in turns to ride the pony while the other kept an eye on the dogs and the fox cub. That meant we generally had to finish up by carrying Jenny, for she would suddenly sit down and nothing on earth would persuade her to move another inch. She loved being carried and really snuggled in. She would lick our hands with her large rough tongue and sometimes she would reach up and give us a big lick right across our noses.

It took her a long time to settle down in the house though. At first she refused to come into the sitting-room. She would draw back into a corner of the kitchen and watch us all suspiciously. Then one day Sophie said, 'Jenny wants my breakfast.'

Sure enough, the cub had come into the dining-room, and she had moved so silently that none of us had noticed her. We threw some bacon rind down for her and she snapped it up and retreated backwards into the corner of the room. When one of the dogs went towards her, she showed her teeth and snarled, a real deep-throated, menacing snarl. The only time she showed the wild side to her nature was when she had food. We tried to break her of this but we never succeeded.

Within three days, Jenny needed no invitation to come into the house. Soon it reached the stage that whenever we had a meal we had three animals in attendance, hoping that a titbit would drop in their direction. Susie, Puppy and Jenny would sit neatly in a row looking up at us expectantly.

When we saw the three of them together like that, it was hard to remember how worried we had been about the dogs being with the cubs. They seemed to have accepted Jenny completely. Susie had taken her welfare to heart and was as tolerant and as good-natured as only a spaniel can be. Puppy, on the other hand, was always on edge when the cub was near her. She would never go to the young fox, but she seemed quite prepared to accept her when Jenny went up to her. Perhaps she only tolerated the cub, but she seemed to wish her no harm. We did not worry any more about leaving the animals together.

It seemed we did not have any need to train Jenny to come when we called because she had no intention of leaving us in the first place. We only bothered to put her out in the run at nights now, or when we were all out. Even then I felt really mean as I shut the door of the run and she sat there looking at me as I walked back across the paddock. She looked so woebegone. It was another matter entirely when I went to get her out. As soon as she heard my voice, she would be out of her sleeping box, wagging her tail so violently that it swung her body from side to side as well. She would come towards me like a rudderless ship. She would run up and sit on my feet, giving little cries of welcome. When I picked her up, she licked each of my fingers in turn with her rough tongue, and if I bent down to talk to her, she would lick my face as well. She still followed Susie about, but if I called her now she would turn straight away and come running to me. She was beautiful.

One day it was really hot and we were all half-dozing in the sunshine. Even the dogs had given up and were stretched out on the grass, and the air was filled with Susie's raucous snores. Suddenly I sat up. Where was Jenny? She was never far away from us and we had grown so used to having the cub around that we did not take much notice of her. Now there was not a sign of her. Even Susie sat up, gazing around her with half-opened bloodshot eyes before she collapsed once more.

Jenny soon appeared. She wandered out of my bedroom, stretching as she came, first her two forelegs, then her back ones. She put back her head and yawned lethargically, then, gently sinking on to her stomach, she dropped her chin on to her paws and looked at me reproachfully.

When I went to bed that night I could not find my pyjamas anywhere. Sophie shouted out that I could borrow her night-dress if I wanted. I found the pyjamas in the end, rolled up into a ball and pushed in a corner under the bed. Jenny had made herself really comfortable there.

After that there was no stopping the fox. She was into my bedroom at every opportunity, and I had no doubt that had she been a little larger, she would have been in the bed rather than beneath it. I put some old clothes down for her, but she would still filch my pyjamas if I forgot to push them right down between the sheets.

Although she liked to get into my bedroom, she liked to know where we were as well. Every so often we would see her pointed nose poking round the door, as if she were just keeping an eye on us. If we were moving about, she would sit on the doorstep watching us, cocking her head first on this side, then on the other, turning one ear round in our direction as we went through to the kitchen, studying our every move. As soon as one of us sat down – it was usually Sophie first – then Jenny would seem assured and trot into her favourite spot under my bed.

Mum did not like the idea of Jenny going into my bedroom at first. She thought that the cub would make a mess in there. Jenny was very good though and in the end Mum became just as fond of the young animal as I was. The only time that Jenny did make a mess indoors was when Sophie forgot she was there and shut her in the kitchen. Sometimes she dribbled a bit, especially when she became really excited, like when Sophie and I came home from school.

Now, as soon as I woke up in the morning, I would go across to the run and let Jenny out. She was always ready to come and would be standing up at the wire with her tail wagging, giving little cries of welcome with her gums drawn back tightly from her teeth. She would often race me back to the house and run straight through the door and up on to my bed, where she would snuggle down into the still-warm patch where I had been lying. If it was still early, and nobody else was up, I would have to push her over to make room for me. She went limp and floppy then, and I would roll her over like a ball. When I got back into bed she would weave her way right under my arms and snuggle against me with little sighs of contentment. Generally she rested her chin under my armpit, and every time she sighed she tickled. Sometimes she rested her chin on my throat, which would have been all right if she had kept it there, but it would creep gradually upwards until I found I had a very cold nose pressed firmly against mine. This was not very helpful for getting back to sleep or doing my homework or whatever I was doing.

She was like a shadow until the minute I left for school. She would come to the gate and see me off, then run back to the house as happy as anything. Sometimes Mum would be in a bit of a hurry herself and ask me to put Jenny back in the run before I went. I never liked doing this. Jenny looked at me so reproachfully when I left that she made me feel guilty.

She would have forgotten by the time I reached home again though. We have never had another animal that has been so pleased to see us as Jenny was. She would be jumping and wagging her tail the minute we appeared. Sometimes she wagged her tail so violently it swung her round full circle. I used to hold out my arms and Jenny would spring right into them. I gave her a big hug before I put her down again. I had to be a bit careful, and quick too, for she would get so excited when she saw us that she made tiny puddles. I did not mind as long as she did not make them on me. Poor Dad was caught out once. He held out his hands and Jenny jumped up into his arms. The only trouble was that he did not put her down quickly enough, and now he has a big yellow stain down the front of his decent shirt.

From the minute I was home Jenny was with me the whole time. She would try to wriggle on to my lap while we were having tea, but this was something we knew we could not allow. She was intelligent enough to know that she had to wait with the dogs and that she would have a titbit at the end of the meal. When she was given hers, Jenny would seize it and snarl over it, although often she was not hungry. Sometimes she would take it out in the garden and bury it rather than eat it. We had a few incidents before Jenny learned that she had to wait for food while we were eating. She pulled the tablecloth off several times. There is nothing more disconcerting than to be enjoying a meal and see the food disappearing at increasing speed over the end of the table, to be attacked viciously by a determined fox cub. She tipped the whole kitchen table over once, scrabbling up the table leg to reach the chocolate cakes Mum had left cooling on the top. I think Susie had given her encouragement then; she certainly helped her finish them off when they landed on the floor.

Jenny was everything that I thought a pet should be, lovable and affectionate, friendly and charming. She was never far away when I was at home. If anything, she was more companionable than the dogs. She was always ready to be petted or go for a walk or just sit beside me when I was doing my homework. She was such an attractive little animal too. At five months she had grown her real ginger coat. Her eyes were bright and alert and her pointed face showed interest in everything that happened around her.

She was wary of the birds though, and kept her distance from them. We were pleased about this because this had been the only worry we had had about her. Would she want the meat the hawks were eating and try to take it from them? Would she ever attack one of the birds? After all, this could well be part of her nature.

It was strange to see how some of her wilder instincts did develop. Her possessiveness over food was always there, and we never tried after those first two or three attempts to disturb her while she was eating. There was also her characteristic of freezing at any unusual noise or sinking low on her haunches if there was something she did not understand.

Then there was the day she suddenly started digging out Mum's flower bed. Mum was not much of a gardener at the best of times, but she did have some roses and marigolds and that sort of thing growing. Jenny went right into the centre and started to dig. Mum shrieked and Dad ran out to see what was happening. He stopped her disturbing the cub. 'Just watch,' he said.

A few seconds later, the young fox dug out a complete nest of mice. Before we could look at them, she had gulped them all down, not even taking the time to chew them but just swallowing them as they were. Jenny dug out several nests after that and finished off the young ones in the same way each time. She never made a mistake but went to the exact spot and started digging.

chapter ten

Jenny liked some people more than she did others. She liked the butcher, but that was cupboard love. He called twice a week and always gave her a piece of chocolate. I do not know if she liked him or the chocolate, but she certainly associated one with the other and always gave him a welcome, running up to him, making little whimpering noises and wagging her tail so enthusiastically from side to side that it made her sway all over the place. She would get so excited that she could not control herself and there would be little spots of liquid left in a line across the floor. The butcher took no notice of that. He would bend down and stroke her and say what a smashing animal she was, until one day she squatted on his shoe and made a puddle on that. He did carry on then, said he did not know why we wanted to keep an animal like that. Anyone could have told us that we would never be able to train a fox. He calmed down a bit but he was never sure of Jenny after that although he always brought her her chocolate, not that he had much choice. Jenny's crying grew more and more persistent so that he had to give it to her before he could hear himself speak.

Jenny did not like the milkman. I think she found him a bit noisy. If he was not whistling he was singing, and he used to rattle the milk bottles in the crates as if they were castanets. As soon as his cart appeared over the top of the hill, Jenny would go to ground, generally under my bed, and would not come out again until the milkman was well on his way to Brandon.

That was how Jenny behaved with most people. Either she was very pleased to see them and made no secret of the fact, or else she would want nothing at all to do with them and would disappear completely until they had gone. Even if she had never seen the people before, she would make up her mind about them as soon as they appeared at the gate, and she never changed it.

There was no rhyme nor reason as to why she decided as she did. Some of the people she liked were people I could not stand, like the pompous old army officer who used to come down from the village and tell us what to do with our own birds and animals and then explain what was wrong with them as well, although he would never have got a prize for accuracy. I was feeding a kestrel once that had its leg in splints, and the colonel, as we called him, leaned right over so that his nose was almost touching the poor bird's beak and said, 'I see it's got a broken wing.' Jenny used to think he was great and would run round and round him when he appeared. The trouble was that he was a hunting man and he did not know what to make of a fox that ran round in circles. He spent so much time stuttering at her that he often forgot why he had come.

Jenny liked the vicar too. The poor man was not a bit fond of animals and I think he must have looked on our house as a kind of penance. Jenny was always pleased to see him, a bit more than I was, because I knew he would want me to do something like read the lesson. The fox seemed to know when he was coming and would often run up the road to meet him. He would find it difficult to make the last few feet to the gate with the effusive welcome he was receiving from Jenny. She danced round his feet and rubbed against his legs and even rolled over on her back offering her tummy to be scratched.

On the other hand, Jenny would not have people like Uncle Charles at any cost, and he really knows about animals and understands them. By the time his car drew up outside the cottage, Jenny would have gone into hiding. I do not think Uncle Charles ever did see her. He is a gamekeeper though, so perhaps some sixth sense warned Jenny that he could represent danger.

Aunt Gertrude wanted to see Jenny one day but she would not come out, not even when we tried to coax her from under the bed with pieces of her favourite chocolate. In the end I moved the whole mattress and Sophie picked her up by her scruff and carried her into the sitting-room. As soon as she was carried through the door, the fox started to struggle and was frantic to get away. Sophie should have let her go really, but she held on to her a bit too long and Jenny scratched her right down the face.

Aunt Gertrude always referred to Jenny as 'that nasty little animal' after that, but she never saw her as she really was, as we used to see her every day.

Another day, when Aunt Gertrude had dropped in for tea, which she did quite a lot, I had gone to get something from my bedroom and Mum had gone to pour out some more tea. Suddenly there was this dreadful scream and a voice calling, 'Help, help, I'm being attacked ... Help!'

We dropped everything and ran to the living-room. There was Jenny sulking behind the settee and Aunt Gertrude standing up in the middle of the room, holding a piece of chocolate cake above her head. We never did find out exactly what happened, although Aunt Gertrude told us several times, but her story was a bit different each time. It seemed that she was just putting the cake to her mouth when Jenny made a dive for it.

It was not the first time Jenny had disgraced herself when we had guests in. One time Dad had some business friends coming in for a meal, and Mum had laid the table with the decent white table cloth and put out the table napkins and set out the places. She had put the salad out in the middle of the table, but when the friends arrived and they went into the dining-room, you should have seen it. The salad had obviously seen better days, and bits of half-chewed beetroot were all over the place. Mum's white tablecloth was

never the same again. There were just stains on the plates where the cold meat had been. There was even a bit of lettuce on top of the picture of Mum's great-grandad, who was supposed to have done something brave in the Indian Mutiny. A couple of glasses were broken on the floor and the glass was mixed with bits of discarded salad. Squirming her way forward through the debris, with cries of pleasure, was Jenny.

I do not think Dad made the favourable impression he had planned. The visitors seemed a bit surprised to come face to face with a fox in the dining-room and did not appear to appreciate it. Mum and Dad did not either. Sophie and I were left to clear up the mess while they went down to a hotel in Grantham for a meal. Jenny had no shame. She was finding bits of the meal that she had hidden in unlikely places for days afterwards.

When we knew we had guests coming, we used to put Jenny back in her run because, as she grew older, she grew more mischievous, more lively and more unpredictable. Dad seemed to think that her mischief was allied to her intelligence. I know some people say that foxes are cunning; well, Dad and I think they are intelligent. I am sure Jenny was. She seemed to understand when we were putting her back in her run, and when we told her, 'No,' which was pretty often, she would sink down on to her haunches immediately and, resting her chin on her forepaws, would gaze at us out of the top of her eyes. Her play was intelligent too. She used to hide things in the same way that the dogs did, but she would always remember where they were and go straight to them when she wanted them again. This was not like the dogs. They seemed to come across anything they had hidden purely by accident.

Jenny liked her toys to do things. A ball that rolled away when she touched it was much more fun than an old bone which would interest the dogs for hours. She would never jump on to a moving ball as the dogs did. Jenny would study it carefully from every angle before she made her 'kill.' Things that had been of some use to somebody interested Jenny much more than toys. A cigarette butt that Dad had thrown away was great. She would spring on it and tear it to pieces. The trouble was when Dad forgot to put a packet of new cigarettes out of reach, which was often, Jenny would always find them and give them the same violent treatment. That always happened at the weekends when Dad could not buy any more. He did not have a good word to say about the fox then.

Once Sophie took her new shoes off and left them in the middle of the floor as usual. When she went to collect them, there was only one there. We found the pieces of the other one torn into shreds and left in a little pile in the corner of the field. Anything like that was good fun to a fox. Sophie was always leaving a sweater on top of Jenny's run. That would have been all right if she had left it all on the top, but often she would leave a sleeve trailing over the edge. That was a real invitation to Jenny, and she would have it away in no time at all. She got Aunt Gertrude's jacket one day. Aunt Gertrude had come in for a cup of tea and left the jacket over the back of her chair. That was too much for Jenny, and she eased it out with all the skill she had developed. Aunt Gertrude had been so busy talking that she had not noticed a thing until it was time to go. I doubt if she would have realized then that it was Jenny that had taken it, if the fox had not got it tangled round her neck and come back into the house with only her head and fore-paws showing. The rest of her was enveloped in this huge jacket and it looked as though she was trying to wear it.

Jenny considered anything that was left lying around good chewing and tearing material, but that was nothing to the fascination anything that moved had for her. Mum had taken a group of girls to Switzerland once, and when she came back she had brought this cuckoo clock. It nearly drove Dad mad. It irritated him. It fascinated Jenny. At first she tried to scramble up the wall to reach the swinging pendulum. Then, when she realized that was impossible, she would sit in the middle of the floor, watching it swing regularly from side to side while her head switched from side to side as well to match its rhythm.

The things she liked best of all were our toys. She had tested most of them out for chewing and tearing and she soon realized it was more than her life was worth to get hold of Sophie's dolls. All the same she did run off with them from time to time, and I am sure she did it for sheer devilment, because she never hurt them.

It was clockwork toys that Jenny loved best. We had bought her a clockwork mouse, and when that wore out we bought a clockwork ladybird and then a frog. She was funny with them. She would look at the toy more and more closely until her nose was almost touching it. She would study it from all angles, running round to the front to have a look, retreating very carefully as it came towards her. Then she would go round to the back of it and then to the side, turning her head almost upside down to make sure that she had really studied it. When the clockwork stopped running, she would sit down or walk off as if she had not been interested in it anyway.

Sophie had a tumbling clown that really intrigued Jenny. It mystified her as well, and she never did learn to trust it, although she tried often enough. We used to wind it up and set it off. Jenny would sit down and look at it suspiciously. Then she would creep forward low along the ground and look at it closely. You could see the puzzlement on her face. First she would turn her head this way and then that. As the clown walked and tumbled sideways, Jenny's nose would get nearer and nearer until it was almost touching the toy. You could see she was getting ready to attack, tensing her muscles ready to leap. That was when the toy would tumble over again, often hitting Jenny on the nose as it rolled. The cub sat back sharply then and you could see the look of injury on her face. Every so often she would decide she had had enough of the clockwork clown and turn her back on it. Curiosity would get the better of her though, and she would cast surreptitious glances over her shoulder at it until it was more than she could bear and she was back at that clown again.

Jenny was funny the first time she saw a butterfly. It was an ordinary cabbage white and it settled in the long grass in front of her. Immediately she sank low on her haunches and began to stalk it. She had nearly reached the butterfly when it fluttered off. The cub sat up and watched it with amazement, but, seeing it settle on a flower a few yards farther on, she began to stalk it warily once more. She was just in a position to pounce when the butterfly flew off again. This time it flew right across the field, weaving a pattern that lasted several minutes. Jenny's patience was at an end. She sprang at it, leaping through the long grass, and for a second she was completely airborne with her body fully extended. It did not get her any nearer. The butterfly had changed direction and was flying lazily towards the cottage. Jenny chased after it, standing up on her hind legs and dabbing at it as it flew. The insect gained height and disappeared over the hawthorn hedge. Jenny returned to a more profitable sport.

chapter eleven

At six and a half months Jenny was almost fully grown
and she was as lively as any puppy of the same age. She was
always ready for a game. If we were having a game of foot-
ball or something like that in the paddock, she would run
after us as if she understood what the game was all about.
I would not have been surprised to see her tackle us for
the ball, she seemed so interested in what was going on.
Susie and Puppy would sit at the edge of the field and watch
in amazement as the cub ran round and round after us.
They would get tired of spectating after a bit and retire to
the garden for a snooze. They could not sleep for long
though, Jenny saw to that.

The two dogs liked to curl up together to sleep, so that
sometimes it was difficult to see where one of them ended
and the other began. Jenny would spring right on top of the
two of them as if they were a springboard, then she would
bounce back and crouch low on her haunches, ready to
jump on them again. She was willing the dogs to play. Sometimes Puppy yapped in temper and curled up again. Jenny
left her alone when she was in one of those moods and con-
centrated on the spaniel. Occasionally Susie growled, but
she generally accepted defeat good-naturedly and got on
to her feet straight away. As soon as she moved, Jenny
would be dancing round her, springing right up on to her
two hind feet in excitement. Then she would invite the dog
to play, prancing round and round, bowing low on the
ground, waiting and springing right up into the air.

It took Susie a long time to rouse herself. She needed a
scratch on this side of her head and a bit of a wash on the
other. Sometimes she would have a sit down or roll over

on to her back so that her legs were extended to the sky. All the time Jenny would be dancing round her inviting her to play. At last the spaniel would pull herself up on to her feet. So would Jenny. The cub would goad the dog then, dashing up to her and pushing her with her sharp little nose, then nipping at her feet quickly and jumping back until Susie was jumping too, as if she had stood on something very hot. Then something of the cub's exuberance would get into the dog, and the two animals would dash round and round the garden like things possessed.

Often Puppy forgot her bad temper and joined in too. The cub was so happy that we all seemed to catch her happiness, and in the end we would all be laughing at them. Dad did not need to cut the lawn that year, except for the edges, because the animals ran round and round so often that the grass did not have a chance to grow in the first place.

Even when she was dashing round like this, if there was an unusual sound Jenny would stop in an instant. It did not matter how far away it was, if it was something out of the ordinary like the noise of a chainsaw down in Matchstick Woods or the grain drier starting up on the farm, Jenny would freeze. It was a fantastic thing to watch. One minute she would be dashing round with complete abandon; the next, she would be as still as a statue. Only the movement of her ears as, independently, they followed the course of the sound, showed that she was alive. Susie and Puppy would carry on the chase for a few more yards; then, when they realized there was not animal there for them to chase, they would stop and look about them uncertainly. The cub always heard the noise before any of us did. She would stand there, poised, alert, until the noise had gone. Then she would resume playing as if there had not been an interruption, and the two dogs would fall obediently into line.

When we were beginning to get dizzy watching them,

Jenny would give in. She would simply stop, lie down on the ground and, rolling over on to her back, dangle her feet in the air as if she were surrendering. At the same time she pulled her lips back, showing her gums and teeth and making funny little crying sounds. It was a most peculiar noise. The three animals would settle down for a rest and we were able to get on with what we had been doing. There was no doubt about it, when Jenny decided to play, everybody forgot everything else. We even began to detect a waistline on Susie. We had tried her on a diet several times, in the hopes of trimming her matronly figure, without success. This extra exercise began to slim her down.

Then the game developed a new twist. The circles in which the cub led the chasing grew bigger and bigger until they went right round the cottage. It gave Mum a real shock the first time it happened. We live outdoors in the summer and we have the dining table out on the veranda. Mum was bringing the dinner out on a tray when the fox dashed by and nearly tripped her over. She had hardly regained her balance when Susie hit her at full speed. Mum said she thought she had been hit in the back of the knees by a bulldozer. She was over, and so was our dinner, potatoes, and carrots and all. The dogs and Jenny got there first and tucked into the food as if they had not eaten for days. Susie did spare the time to lick Mum across the face, but Sophie said that was to collect a stray piece of potato rather than to show any affection. Mum was careful how she came out of the front door after that, especially if she was carrying anything.

Once or twice, visitors were taken aback when they came to our house and saw one animal after another dashing past them. The vicar said it had taken him five minutes to knock on the door once, because every time he reached towards the knocker, another animal had dashed past his feet. The man who was trying to sell brooms had a similar reception. Mum said she did not know why he was so upset. It was not as if any of the animals tried to hurt him. When she answered the door, the man began to talk, but he had hardly finished a sentence when Jenny dashed by, running over his feet. The man stopped what he was saying and stared in the direction that she had gone. He started again, only to be disturbed by Puppy, who dashed by at a similar rate of knots. When Susie panted by on the same circuit, blundering into his brooms and knocking them all over the place, the man looked at Mum and said, 'I do meet some peculiar people.' Then, gathering his brooms together, he marched out of the gate and we never saw him again. Mum did not mind really, because she never buys anything at the door anyhow.

Jenny developed yet another angle. She used to get the two dogs running round and round the cottage after her; then, when they were both going at full speed, she would go and sit on the front doorstep and watch them running by. They would keep going for several more circuits before they realized they were not chasing anything. When they stopped running and started to look around, Jenny would spring up and start dashing round the house again. She generally ran in the same direction, but sometimes, just to muddle the dogs, she would turn round and go the other way. That did cause problems. Poor Susie was much too fat to make a quick turnabout. She would sit down and still be sitting there thinking about the matter when the other two dashed by her again. Sometimes, particularly when the dogs had been reluctant to start playing in the first place, Jenny would get them rushing round and round in great excitement and then, when they were not looking, go into my bedroom, curl up in her favourite spot on my bed and go to sleep.

Jenny was attracted to all dogs. She did not show the same likes and dislikes with dogs that she did with people. She loved them all. Anybody who came to our house with a dog would be greeted by an excited, crying, exuberant fox cub. Jenny herself received a mixed reception. Most people seemed to think she would harm their pets in some way, even if she was not a quarter of their size. I do not think anyone who came with a dog really welcomed Jenny in the way they seemed to think we should welcome their pet. Generally they took their dogs outside or put them in their cars.

Mum and Dad were pleased. I suppose people thought we were fond of all animals, which, in a way, we are. But other people's dogs were a real problem. The birds we had in soon learned to accept our own dogs, but if a strange one went near them they would get so upset that Dad worried about them having fits. Weeks of work could be undone in a few minutes in that way. People used to say, 'The dog will be all right,' when we mentioned the birds, or, 'He wouldn't hurt a fly.' That was not the point. Their presence was enough to upset a wild bird.

One day a man called with his dog, and when we did not answer the door immediately, he started to walk round the garden. We had three pairs of owls on eggs and they all deserted. That was a real disappointment because it is very hard to get these wild, injured birds to a state where they will breed in captivity.

Jenny soon sorted out those problems. Once people realized the reception they were likely to have if they brought a dog in, they made considerable efforts to keep the animals out.

It was not only people who brought their dogs to the house that were reluctant to meet Jenny. People we met when we were out for a walk showed the same attitude. It was nothing unusual to be walking up the lane with Jenny and the dogs and see somebody who was exercising his own dog turn smartly round and go back the way he had come.

I shall never forget the time the four of us came round the corner and met the lady who lives up the lane waiting for the bus with her dog. She had a Pekingese, which only

seemed half-dog to me at the best of times. Jenny probably thought he was a ball anyway. He seemed to be more hair than dog, and half of that was gathered in little bundles and tied with blue ribbons. The fox made straight for him. The Peke was so surprised he seemed to fall over backwards. That was good fun and Jenny started to dance round him, inviting him to play in exactly the same way that she invited our own two dogs. The lady tried to wave her away and pick up her own dog at the same time. It seemed that he did not want to be picked up. He started running round and round with the fox, yapping all the time like one of those squeaky children's toys. He could certainly move, and he gave Jenny a run for her money. He gave his mistress a run as well; she was chasing after him trying to pick him up. There was Peke chasing fox and lady chasing Peke. I tried to calm her down and told her that Jenny would not hurt her dog, but she did not seem to hear me.

Then Jenny found the puddle where the ditch had over-flowed. She went right through it, followed by the Peking-ese, who came out of it a decidedly different colour. So did the lady. She made a final grab at her pet and seemed to dive headfirst into the muddy water. The fox and dog ran round and round her, going through the puddle on each circuit as if the lady was not sitting in the middle of it. I helped her up but all she would say was, 'Oh dear, oh dear.'

I picked her dog up for her too. He was so out of condi-tion, he was panting like a steam engine. The lady was so pleased to see him that she did not seem to notice that he was dirty. She hugged him as if she had not seen him for years. She did not seem to notice the mud on her own nose or the colour of her own stockings and coat. At that moment the bus came over the hill. She climbed into it with-out a backward glance at Jenny, who was sitting there as good as gold.

Sometimes Jenny suddenly became tired and just stopped where she was. Often that would be when we were right over the fields and I had to carry her home. Although she was not very big, she weighed more than enough for her size.

She became tired in some pretty funny places. One day we had builders in to replace the tiles on the roof. We had all gone out shopping and when we came home they were still there.

'You're working late,' Mum said when she got out of the car.

'Well, it's a bit awkward,' the man said. 'I can't get in my car.'

Mum looked at him and looked at the car. It seemed all right to her.

'I know it sounds daft,' the man said, 'but there's a fox in the driving seat and it won't get out.'

Sure enough, there was Jenny. The man had left his

sweater on the seat. It was just the kind of bed that Jenny appreciated.

Another time a man called at the door. He was trying to sell magazines and that sort of thing. Since we never buy anything at the door, Mum shut it in his face, very firmly because he was rather persistent. She was very annoyed when she went out half an hour later and discovered him still standing there. She felt sorry though when she found out what had happened. He had put his case down on the ground and opened it up, whereupon Jenny had promptly got in it. He had tried to push her out but Jenny obviously thought he was being friendly. She had wagged her tail and put up her head, pulling back her gums so that her teeth were showing. She often did this when she was pleased to see somebody; it was her way of greeting them. When the man saw her teeth though, he thought she was threatening him. He did not realize she was trying to be friendly.

Jenny did like to climb into things, especially if there was something soft in the bottom. Aunt Gertrude took her home by mistake one day. Dad always reckoned she carried a purse that was big enough to hold the kitchen sink. It was certainly big enough to hold Jenny. It was not until she was getting ready for bed that night and wanted something from her bag that she felt the soft, warm fur, and when it moved, she knew what had happened. She never let us forget either.

Sometimes Jenny did get into unexpected places. The vicar came to see us one day. Mum invited him in and asked him to sit down. He got up twice as quickly as he sat down. In fact, one could say he shot out of the chair. At the same time Jenny started to run round and round the room. It seems she had been asleep on the chair and the vicar had thought she was a cushion and sat on her.

One night, Mum went to bed late. We all knew it was late because no sooner had she got there than she sprang out again with such a scream that she woke us all up, the neighbours as well. Apparently she had gone to bed and put her feet down between the sheets. That was when they met something warm and soft. Before she had time to do anything, the something moved and so did she.

It was Jenny of course. I thought Mum had put her into the run that night, and she thought I had put her away. Jenny had taken matters into her own hands and put herself away, in Mum's bed. Mum made such a fuss about that you would have thought she had been hurt. As Dad pointed out, it was Jenny who must have had the bigger shock, meeting Mum's feet like that when she thought she was in a nice peaceful spot.

chapter twelve

It was like any other afternoon that day. Sophie and I got off the school bus. As we walked up from the corner, Puppy hurled herself at us with her usual enthusiasm, jumping up at Sophie and knocking her backwards so that she sat down on the grass verge. Susie came down more placidly, her short apology for a tail shaking like a quivering jelly. As we reached the back door, Jenny came across the room, wagging from side to side and giving little yelps of welcome. She would have sat down on my foot if she could have kept her tail still, but every time she lowered herself a little, her tail seemed to wag a little more strongly and she was propelled forwards farther. So she wove an erratic path round us, and in the end I had to pick her up. She licked me right down my face. Her tail was still wagging, which made all of her wriggle so I was forced to put her down again.

Sophie had seen the cakes. Mum could only just have taken them from the oven, because they were still warm. We took one each and gave a bit to Jenny. She gobbled it up and looked expectantly for more. We took another one each just as Mum came in with the washing. 'My cakes,' she exclaimed.

Well, we all started laughing and Jenny joined in the excitement too, dashing round and round giving high-pitched little barks. Then she leaped down the step into the garden and ran round and round near the laurel bushes. She looked so happy and kittenish that we laughed at her.

Mum was putting the kettle on and, while she was not looking, I eased another cake from the plate. Suddenly there was this quick sharp noise and then silence. My hand halted in mid-air. Was it a bark or a yelp? I could not describe it but I knew something was wrong. Mum turned round too but Sophie carried on, talking away.

I reached the garage first but Mum was right behind me. Jenny, dear little Jenny, was lying there, feebly moving her front legs. The two dogs were there as well. Puppy was standing tense and alert, her tail curled up over her back. Susie was nuzzling the small brown body.

'Oh no.' I could not move. I was completely horror-struck. Mum ran forward and pushed the dogs away. She picked up the cub. Even as she lifted her, I could see Jenny arch her back and lift her head, tightening her gums until she showed the rows of small sharp teeth.

Mum ran indoors with the fox in her arms and laid her gently on the hearthrug in front of the fire. Sophie had not realized anything had happened and had followed us to the door chattering happily away. When she saw Jenny, she stopped in mid-sentence and a look of consternation, then horror spread across her face.

'I'll get the vet,' Mum said.

I knew then that it was too late. There was nothing I could do. I stood there and I kept saying, 'Don't let her be dead. Don't let her be dead.' I looked at the little animal lying there. Mum was talking on the phone. When she came in, she said, 'I was lucky to catch the vet. He was on his way out when I phoned. He's coming over straight away.'

I knew it would not be any good, that nobody could do anything for Jenny now. I did not want to see the vet. I did not want to see anyone. Taking my old jacket off the peg, I ran out across the fields. Puppy came too. I did not want her. I did not want to see her ever again. I knew it was Puppy that had killed Jenny. I could not prove it, but I knew. The way she had been standing when we ran into the garage was enough for me. There had been no sign of injury on the fox, there were no cuts or bites, but I knew, from the way she had put back her head, that her back had been broken. I had seen Puppy kill a hare and a couple of rabbits in exactly the same way.

I tried to push Puppy back home. I shouted and kicked out at her but she would not go back. She stuck to me like glue. Even when a couple of hares got up from almost beneath our feet, she stayed as close to me as my own shadow. Every time I swung my hand down she would reach up and lick it. The more I tried to push her back, the closer she seemed to stick. It seemed that she thought she could make up for what she had done by really staying with me.

I must have walked miles, right over the fields and through the woods. I hated those woods but they fitted my mood that day. They had been so beautiful until the farmer had cleared them. It took little more than a month to fell those great, gaunt oaks. They must have looked over that land for more than two centuries; a couple of hours was enough to destroy each one. Sophie and I had watched them grub up the useless stumps with the huge relentless machines and tow them into the still-living part of the woods. There they lined the path, fifty or sixty of them, black and dark and rotting. I hated to see them and I hardly went up there because I could remember what those woods had looked like in the height of summer. No farmer's profits or rows of militant barley could ever justify the destruction of that beauty.

We went right through to the badger sets. We often used to sit up there in the summer twilight watching the cubs play. Somebody had been there too. All the entrances were stuffed up with stones and tins and bits of paper. Wasn't anything going to be right? I sat on the ground and looked back the way I had come. I wanted to be alone, but Puppy crawled up towards me on her belly and pushed her nose beneath my arm.

Perhaps it was not her fault after all. Perhaps it was

too much to expect a dog like a whippet to accept a basically wild animal into its home. However tame Jenny had seemed to us, it did not change the fact that she was a wild animal. We may have dulled the wilder side of her nature, but those characteristics were still there, like her digging up the nests of mice or her behaviour over food or the way she went to ground. Perhaps it was too much to expect Puppy to accept this, particularly when she belonged to a hunting breed herself. I put my hand down and stroked her head. Immediately she wormed herself up into my lap, where she settled down with a little sigh, just as she always did. Was this what had been the matter? Had she been jealous? Had I been giving too much attention to Jenny and leaving Puppy out?

Then I heard Dad's voice shouting as he came down the lane. Looking at my watch, I saw that I must have been sitting there for more than three hours. I got up and went towards him. He was pleased to see me. 'Come on, lad,' he said.

It was as much as I could do to go towards the house. Nobody could understand the effort it took me. When I reached Dad, he said, 'We think she's going to be all right. The vet's only just gone.'

I looked at him, hardly able to believe the words.

'You mean she's not dead?'

Before he could give me an answer, I was running back to the house as fast as I could.

chapter thirteen

Jenny did not die. At times in the following weeks, I wondered if it would have been best if she had done so. For the first two days she lay in a box by the fire. She was not interested in anything, not even food. Mum would not let us touch her or disturb her at all. She said Jenny had had a bad shock and must be kept quiet. On the third day, Jenny put her head up and looked round. She was beginning to take an interest. She lapped up the milk and glucose we gave her and went back to sleep. She really did seem to be getting better.

Then Mum put her on the rug so that she could clean out her box. She had not wanted to move her until then, not even to clean out the box. Jenny tried to stand. She managed it, but only for a second. Her hind legs were so weak that she swayed from side to side and collapsed on to the floor. She struggled to get back on to her feet, only to collapse once again.

'She can't walk,' Sophie said.

I stood and stared. What could I say?

We got the vet up again, and I stayed to hear what he said that time. I was sure he would say there was nothing else we could do, that it was not fair to keep her alive. He did not say anything like that though.

'She's bruised her spine,' he said. 'There's no permanent injury there. She'll be all right but it'll take a long time. The trouble is that blood gets into the spinal cord and that's what causes the damage, but it's only temporary. She'll be quite all right as long as you're prepared to take the trouble nursing her.'

'Of course we are,' Mum said without even asking how

much nursing was involved. The vet gave us some anti-biotics for the fox and said he would call and see her again when he was passing.

Day after day Jenny lay there. We kept trying to convince ourselves that she was getting better, but we knew really that there was no improvement at all. At first, she tried to get on to her feet, and it was pitiful to see her struggling upright, only to balance shakily for a few seconds before she fell to the ground again. Then she did not seem to want to try any more. She was eating all right and she had re-covered her possessive attitude where food was concerned. Because she could not get on to her feet, she could not make a mess in the proper way, and she became really dirty round her hindquarters. Mum was always washing her, too often really, because her hair started to come out and she got very sore there.

There was the smell too and the flies. It was a very hot summer and it was impossible to control either of them. Although we had not noticed when Jenny had been fit, now we could not ignore the pungent foxy smell which seemed to taint everything. Sophie used to pour lavender water over things to try to hide the smell. I began to wonder if the foxy odour was not preferable, especially when I took my foot-ball kit out of the bag at school and found she had poured perfume all over that as well. You should have heard what my friends said. The trouble was that it was almost impos-sible to get rid of the foxy smell. If you washed anything that smelled of it, the water seemed to strengthen the smell rather than the reverse.

Obviously we could not continue keeping Jenny in the house, so we fitted her up in the conservatory which led out of the kitchen. Even that proved too much, and Dad had to modify the run out in the paddock so that we could move it on to fresh ground every time the ground it was standing on became soiled.

I used to go over and see Jenny before I went to school

and as soon as I got home in the evening. I hated seeing her lying there, especially when I remembered her as she used to be. Her front half seemed lively enough. She would lie in the run with her head up, looking pert and interested in everything. It was her hindquarters that were useless.

Then one day I went over to see her before I went down for the bus and she wagged her tail. It did not register immediately, not until I was walking across the field.

'She wagged her tail!' I could not help saying it at the top of my voice, and I dashed back to make sure that I had not made a mistake. Sure enough, when I called her name, she wagged her tail. Jenny was getting better.

Her recovery was miraculously quick after that. When I got home that evening, she was standing up in her run and she even walked a few shaky steps when I opened the door. By the end of the week, it was almost impossible to tell that she had been hurt at all, except for a certain stiffness in her movement. For four weeks she had been pathetic, and we had wondered if we were doing right to keep her alive. Then, overnight, she seemed to get suddenly better. She started to get her proud looks back and her glossy coat.

She was never quite the same again, although I tried to think she was. I do not know whether Jenny was wary of the dogs or we ourselves tended to keep them apart, but the old friendship between Susie, Puppy and Jenny had gone for ever. Jenny never followed the dogs now. We would have been worried had she done so, because as soon as Puppy saw the fox out of her run, the hairs on the back of her neck began to bristle and she became tense and alert. We could not have trusted the whippet.

Jenny did not come into the house at all now, although we did try to encourage her. She seemed happier out in her own run and went back there rather than follow us across the paddock when we called her. Perhaps it was just as well. Her glands had fully developed and she had this strong, musky fox smell that got into everything. We did

not notice it when she was with us, but when she had gone
the smell seemed to hit us in an overpowering wave. The
dogs seemed to be much more interested in me when we
had Jenny, and I am sure it must have been the smell that
I was carrying round on my clothes which attracted them.
One day we did a cross-country run at school, and by the
time I got back to the gym, I had eight dogs following me.

Jenny was not as lively during the day. She would wake
up as the sun set and want to get up then. The worst thing
was that she no longer wanted to be with me. She would
not sit on my lap while I did my homework or come into
my bedroom with me when I had my records on; all she
wanted to do was to get back to her own familiar run. She
would wag her tail when she saw me, but she did not give
me the same old effusive greetings that I loved. The only
person she was really pleased to see was Mum, and I think
that was because it was always Mum that fed her and she
associated her with food.

When we let her out in the evenings, Jenny would run across the field and disappear almost immediately. She blended in so well with the background of hedges and trees that it was almost impossible to see her. We would have no idea where she was unless we saw the movement of the long grass. Sometimes a blackbird would give its strident warning call, which would be echoed and re-echoed by half the other occupants in the hedge, and we would guess that it was Jenny that had disturbed them. Generally she would simply melt into the scene and we would have no idea where to look for her.

Mum had her secret weapon though, the food dish. As soon as Mum brought her dinner out, Jenny would appear from the most unlikely places. Food was her great weakness.

But one day she did not come back.

Dad was really worried. 'She isn't like an ordinary fox,' he said. 'We knew that dog fox we had wouldn't stay in the vicinity, that as soon as he could he'd put as much space between us and himself as possible because he was wild. Jenny's been taught to accept us, and she's likely to stay around. We know she's been getting wilder every day. Oh yes we do,' he added as I started to interrupt him. 'Jenny is a wild animal and there's no knowing what her reaction will be if she comes face to face with any of the birds in the garden. It frightens me to think of the damage she could do if she comes back when we're not around. A determined fox can get into anything, and that fox is determined enough. We'll have to take it in turns sitting up all night. Somebody's got to be here when she comes back.'

Can anywhere be more strange than one's own back garden at night? I knew the cottage was only a matter of yards away, but I felt in a world apart from it, completely enveloped in my own area of darkness. Yet the garden was not completely dark. It was the time when the colours were fading, when the last shades of green were melting into the oblivion of dark and light. The moon rose slowly, and there were deep shadows from which strange noises, scratches and rustles, emanated. Even familiar objects acquired a different character in this world of dark and shade. The birds, particularly the owls, which were so much a part of our lives, seemed to become all-powerful as they sat in their aviaries and moved their heads to look towards something that had attracted their attention.

I knew every inch of that garden, yet in the night it was a place that was totally strange to me. Even the apple tree we climbed and swung from in the daytime seemed to suggest something sinister with its twisted branches.

I hoped Mum would not be long. I know it sounds silly to be scared in one's own back garden. I was not really frightened, more uneasy. Far away I heard the engine of an aeroplane, and as it died away, there was complete and utter silence. It only lasted for a second or two, for as my ears became accustomed to the stillness, I heard the other noises, the ones that are always there and that one tends to ignore among the more familiar everyday sounds. There was rustling and squeaking in the hedgerows and the soft noises of nesting birds.

As I walked quietly along the line of aviaries, Boz, one of the tawny owls, leaned forward and hooted a welcome right into my ear. I nearly jumped out of my skin. It seemed a signal for all the owls to join in, first our own in the aviaries and then the wild birds farther down the lane. As the staccato note of the little owls died away, the garden returned to its former stillness.

Once more I waited for any tell-tale sign that would let me know Jenny was about, but there was nothing, just complete and utter silence. I sat down with my back against the apple tree and waited. I wondered why all the eagle owls were staring at the same patch of garden that had attracted their attention half an hour earlier. They were looking at exactly the same place. It was a patch of bramble and nettles that we had left completely untouched. We called it the jungle. The owls were still staring at it intently, so I walked up there very quietly. I lay down on my tummy and cautiously opened the brambles. I eased myself into them a little way, and, as I did so, I found myself face to face with Jenny. I do not know which of us was more surprised.

I think she was pleased to see me. She whimpered and wagged her tail. I did not give her time to change her mind. I caught hold of her by the scruff of her neck and eased the two of us backwards out of that bramble patch, which was much harder than getting into it and a good deal more painful. Dad came out for his turn 'on watch' just as I was walking across the grass. 'Am I pleased to see her,' he said. 'I dread to think of the damage she could have done.'

I was just as pleased to see my bed. I cannot remember a time when it was more welcome than that night.

chapter fourteen

Poor Jenny. She had to be restricted from then on. We never let her out again unless we were sure that she was hungry and that the smell of food was certain to tempt her back. Even then she was a bit of a worry. She began to do the one thing that Mum and Dad had been afraid of from the beginning. She started to show an interest in the birds in the garden, particularly those that we tethered on the lawn during the day. I think it was the lines by which they were tethered that first attracted her. She would lie on her tummy and dab at them like a kitten dabs at a ball of wool. She realized very quickly that there was a bird on the other end of the line, and if it became worried or flapped its wings, Jenny was alert and poised ready to spring immediately. Luckily we saw her when she started behaving like this, so we made sure that every bird was well out of her reach and the tethered birds were back in the mews before we let Jenny out each evening.

It was difficult keeping an eye on her all the time. She was so quick and unpredictable. Often I would watch her play in one part of the garden. If I let my attention wander for an instant, Jenny would be somewhere completely different. She also had this ability to freeze in an instant, so that she merged completely with the grass or hedge or whatever was behind her. Sometimes I would be staring right at her and yet I would be unable to pick her out, she was so well camouflaged.

Then, one day, she really did blot her copybook.

Several months earlier we had been sent a couple of chickens. Somebody had decided they did not want them any more and had thought we would be able to use them for food. They were in a sack, and when we opened it, we found they were still alive. Of course, instead of providing food, they became more things to feed, and it was not long before they began to pay their rent with daily eggs. They were so little trouble that we did not take a lot of notice of them except to throw them out a handful of corn each morning.

One evening there was such a noise outside we wondered whatever was happening. I dashed round to the back garden. Mum was there first. There was no need to ask what had happened. A line of white chicken feathers led us down the path, and we met Jenny coming towards us with the white hen held firmly in her mouth. Jenny had the bird by the bottom of her neck in some way and the rest of her body slung over her shoulder. The hen's head was free though, and she was protesting at the top of her unmusical voice. There was no mistaking the pride Jenny was taking in her acquisition as she high-stepped along the path in front of us. She would not let go of that chicken, and both Mum and I had to hold her. It took all our strength to prise her mouth open and let the hen free. The hen fluttered off with a great display of indignation and, except for the loss of some feathers, seemed little the worse for wear. The experience must have upset her though, for it put her off egg-laying and we did not have our regular supply for several weeks.

When we let Jenny out the next night, she went right to the spot where she had found the hen the day before and began to stalk through the bushes. I watched her as she moved carefully and stealthily as any wild fox I have ever seen. Her nose was twitching the whole time. She had certainly got the scent of our two hens.

I do not know if the blow she had had from the whippet had caused this change in her behaviour or whether this side of her character was so inbred that it would have developed in any case. There was no doubt at all, however, that she was fast becoming Jenny the fox, rather than Jenny the pet.

Then we had a visit from another fox. It had got into one of the aviaries. Mum found the hole when she went out to feed the birds before breakfast. She ran back to the house shouting. Sophie and I were just getting up and we ran out, half in our pyjamas and half in our clothes, wondering whatever had happened. Dad was out already looking at the hole. There was no doubt that it was a fox that made it. There were the marks where the animal had dug its way in, and several ginger hairs had caught on the wire.

Of the five tawny owls that should have been in that aviary, there were only two left. They were not much help either when I went in to mend the hole. They both tried to sit on my head and nibble my ear. I know they were only trying to be friendly, but it's a bit awkward when you are nearly upside down trying to thread wire through the mesh. It was not until I was in the first lesson at school that morning that I discovered one of them must have lifted its tail when it had been sitting there and left a white streak down the back of my head.

Mum thought the fox had taken the other three owls, but Dad calmed her down. He said there were no signs of a struggle. There were no feathers lying about, and it was much more likely that the fox had come to steal the food that had been left in there and that the owls themselves had found their way out of the hole it had made. We need not have worried. All three owls were back on the roof of the aviary that night trying to get back in. They led us a dance though, because they would not let us pick them up but, in their attempts to get back into their home, kept dive-bombing us and anyone else who happened to call. In the end we took the roof off the aviary and put it back on when they had all come back several days later.

We were worried that the fox would come back that night. Foxes generally do return to an easy food supply. We had a gamekeeper that lived at the end of the lane, and Dad told me to run up and ask him what he suggested we do.

The keeper was sitting in his kitchen fastening his gaiters when I called at his cottage. I had to shout the message at him several times before he started to understand. He always said he was deaf, but Dad said he was as cunning as a fox himself and could understand what he wanted to hear. He was always quick enough to answer if anyone offered him a pint at the pub. He said he would go down and look at the situation and, although I took the shortcut across the fields, he was back there before me.

The keeper was a fascinating person to watch. He was a little, inoffensive man who reminded me of a weasel when he got on the track of something that disturbed his pheasants. Now he was walking round the paddock, his nose twitching just like Jenny's did when she got the scent of something.

'Aye, it's a fox all right,' he said, drawing a red hair off the wire. He held it up and added, 'Look at that white tip on the end there. There's only the one thing that can be. That's your fox all right, and if it's had an easy feed it'll be back again. They're clever animals, foxes,' There was no doubting the grudging admiration in his voice as he said that.

'How are we going to stop it? We can't have foxes getting in here.'

'You'll have to wait for it with a twelve-bore. It's the only way.'

'It's too risky with all these birds around like this.'

'I'll tell you what. Foxes don't like paraffin. Have you got any o' that? They won't cross a line o' paraffin. You paint a line right round your place. That'll keep him out.'

'But paraffin evaporates,' I interrupted.

'Aye, that's the trouble with it. You can soak pieces of newspaper with it and put those right round. That's what

I do on the rearing field. It stays on that longer. Mind you, you'll have to keep doing it.'

'Do you think Jenny's attracting them in?' Mum asked.

'Could well be. Could well be,' the keeper muttered.

Dad had talked about this from the minute that we had had the foxes. Foxes will visit one another in the wild, and he had wondered if they would visit those in captivity as well.

First of all we had to deal with the immediate problem. We poured paraffin into a bucket. Sophie screwed up balls of newspaper and soaked them in it. Then I strung them right round the part of the garden where the aviaries were. We painted a line on the ground as well for good measure. I suppose those pieces of newspaper hanging there did look funny. Most of the people who called made remarks about it, especially the butcher, who insisted Sophie and I were experimenting with some kind of Christmas decorations. It did the trick though. We did not have any visits from unwanted foxes.

Jenny's presence was a worry. We felt sure that she had attracted the wild one in and were frightened that she would attract others. She decided the issue herself. She started pacing, walking up and down the run, up and down, as if she wanted to be out. Mum could not bear it. She is not keen on seeing animals in captivity unnecessarily, but watching one that was basically wild, as Jenny was, that paced in its run and was obviously unsettled, was more than she could stand. She really worried about it. So we began to make plans to release Jenny to the wild.

chapter fifteen

It was not easy to find anywhere to let Jenny go. They hunt twice a week in the season, and we had not brought her up so that she could provide easy prey for the hounds. Dad was convinced the situation would never arise. He thought that Jenny was far too cunning to allow herself to be caught and that within twenty-four hours she would start to adapt to the countryside and her own natural place in it. Mum and Sophie and I were not so sure. We did not want to take the risk and wanted to find somewhere where the hunt did not go. We also had to find somewhere away from poultry farms or anywhere where she could do damage.

Tom had had to be shot. We all felt sad about that, and so had the people who had taken him from us and looked after him. He had always had that independent streak in him although he had been really attractive too. He had shown all the same signs that Jenny had developed as she grew wilder. He had started to return to his run later and later, but his new owners had not worried about him because he was always there when they got up in the morning, and they simply had to go out and shut the door of his run. They did not recognize the danger sign. Tom never wanted the food they put out for him each day. Obviously he was eating elsewhere. They were pleased because they thought he was learning to cope for himself in the wild. They did not stop to think how.

They did not worry about him until reports started coming in about a fox that was getting into hen houses at the other end of the village. It was getting in in such a cunning way that a lot of people doubted if it was a fox at all. The way that the hens were killed or left maimed and dying was typical of the way a fox kills, but this one seemed to be able to lift latches and nose doors open, which is what one would expect from a dog rather than a fox. Of course Tom had been brought up with dogs and had learned some of their tricks. He had been able to undo catches from an early age. The fox in the village was not like a wild fox either in that it did not return to its kill. Farmers waited up night after night, but he did not go back. Instead he moved on to the next place where hens were kept. He ranged as far as four miles in one night.

Tom's new owners determined to keep Tom in to see if the killing stopped, but I think in their heads they knew it was Tom that was causing the damage. He had been brought up to have no fear of humans and human situations. It was too late to do anything about it. Tom's chance of life had run out.

His new owner had hens of his own. He also bred peacocks. His only doubt about Tom being responsible for killing the livestock in the area was the fact that his own birds had not suffered. Tom seemed to take no notice of them. But one morning, when the owner got up, he knew that Tom had struck at home. There was a sea of feathers across the lawn, and sitting in the middle of them, was Tom. His mask was a mass of blood and feathers and he brushed them nonchalantly aside with his forepaw as he tucked into the meal in front of him. His owner recognized his prey as one of his own peacocks, the white one that was the pride of his collection. He did not have to look beyond the lawn to see that this was not the only victim, for a trail of dead and dying birds and scattered feathers showed the path that the fox had taken. The owner took his twelve-bore from the shelf and shot the fox from his bedroom window.

We did not want Jenny to go anywhere in the region where she was likely to cause such damage. We wanted her to be released in an area where she could adapt to a diet similar to that of wild foxes. The story of Tom made Mum even more determined that Jenny would be released well out of reach of our own home. She really worried about the damage a tame fox could do to the other animals in the centre.

We found the ideal place by chance. A new landowner had moved into the area and had started by refusing the hunt the right to go on his land. He owned thousands of acres and we knew we could find a good spot for Jenny there. We used to go and watch badgers in one of his woods. This particular spot was three miles from the nearest village, too far for Jenny to go to make mischief, we thought. It seemed just right. Dad and I spent the whole of Sunday there investigating the area, and it seemed to have everything that a fox would need.

Foxes were there already. We found their den easily. There was no mistaking it for the badger set (which was higher up amongst the trees), because, before we got right up to the hole, we could smell that pungent, foxy smell with which we had become familiar. We decided to fix Jenny up about three hundred yards from the den. If we put her any nearer, the foxes would probably drive her off, but if they could become used to her gradually, they were likely to accept her. They are companionable animals to their own kind.

Dad had built a new box for Jenny at the end of her run and she had soon grown used to it. The idea was that we could take the whole thing off when we were ready to let her go and put it in the hole that Dad and I had dug out in the wood. Then she would have something familiar to which she could return.

We had prepared everything very carefully, and one Sunday morning we took her up to the woods to release her. I went with very mixed feelings. Part of me did not want her to go, yet I knew it was the best for her, that she should have the chance of the life of freedom that was right for a fox.

Dad slid the special lid that he had made over the front of her new den, and we lifted the whole thing out of the run. It was heavy and it needed all four of us to move it. We really had trouble getting the box into the van we had borrowed to take it across to the wood, especially as it dropped on Dad's toe while we were getting it there. You would have thought his toe had dropped off from the fuss he made.

We had the same difficulty getting it out when we reached the wood. We managed it in the end and carried it up to the place we had prepared. The box slipped easily right down into the hole we had made, and unless you knew it was there, you would not have noticed it, it fitted in so well and blended in with the elder and young ash that were growing there.

I pulled the door out and stood back to see how Jenny was going to react. She was sitting there pert and alert and not one bit worried. The journey there had upset us more than it had upset her. She cocked her head to one side and then to the other as if she were summing up the situation. She turned one ear in one direction and turned the other a different way. She sat there watching us and we stood there watching her.

'Well,' said Dad, 'we're not going to achieve much standing here like this. Come on. We can come back this evening and see how she is. I'm ready for my dinner.'

'That reminds me,' Mum said. 'We must get Jenny's dinner. Run down and get it, Sophie. I put it under the front seat.'

Sophie was back in no time at all with the dish that was so familiar to the fox. It was the one we had used for the foxes from the beginning. Mum had already put Jenny's favourite meal in it. Now she took the dish from Sophie and went towards the fox, meaning to put the food down in front of her.

That was when Jenny moved. She ran between us so

103

quickly that we did not realize what was happening, down the path the way we had come, and on to the road. There she sat.

'She wants to go back in the car,' Sophie said.

We went down after her. I think Sophie was right. Jenny was sitting beside the car as if she were waiting for someone to open the door for her. The end of the story might have been different had not another car turned the corner at the bottom of the lane and come grinding up the hill towards us. That was when Jenny moved again. She started to run, and she ran until she was out of sight, running effortlessly up the hill towards the village.

Mum was worried about her, but Dad said Jenny would be all right. She knew where the box was, and animals nearly always come back to the spot from which they have been released. He did not think Jenny would be any different from any of the others in that respect. We would go back in the evening, and he had no doubt at all that we would find Jenny back in the den we had fixed up for her.

But we did not, not that evening or any of the other times we went up there. We went back after tea, but the box was empty and the food had not been touched. Mum went up to the woods every day for three weeks, and that whole time there was no sign at all that Jenny had gone back there. She put food out there regularly but it was never touched, except for the times that Susie managed to sneak back and lick the dish clean. There was never any sign that the box had been slept in either.

We hoped that Jenny was all right. It was all we could do.

chapter sixteen

I missed Jenny a lot. We had other animals and birds coming in, but none of them could be quite like Jenny. She had been something special. She continued being something special too.

We had not seen or heard anything about her although we often thought about her. We went round the woods, up through the village and across the fields beyond it, but there was no sign of her at all. It was as if she had vanished. Then Mum opened the paper one day, and there was a picture of Jenny in the middle of the front page, a large picture of her tucking into a dish of food, with two big Alsatians sitting back watching her.

We knew it was Jenny; it was the sort of thing she would do.

Beneath the picture was the story of the fox that had invited itself to dinner. When a lady had taken out a meal for the dogs, the fox had simply come along too. The dogs had been so surprised to see her that they had sat back and let her help herself. That cunning fox must have gone straight up there the minute we had let her go, for the day they gave as the first time she had appeared was the same day that we had let her go. We had been worrying about her, wondering how she was coping in the wild, while all the time she was living off the fat of the land. There was no doubt about that. The lady gave a list of the foods that the fox preferred, and top of the list was chocolate and breakfast cereals, the two things Jenny had always enjoyed most. It seemed she was turning up punctually every evening for her meal.

Mum and Sophie and I went up to see the old lady. We were rather hesitant about going in at first because her two Alsatians were barking and jumping up and looking really fierce, but when we opened the gate and walked down the path, they proved to be just as soft as our own two dogs.

I think the lady thought we had come to try to take Jenny away, because she was not at all friendly at first. When Mum explained that she only wanted to make sure that the fox was not a nuisance and that there was no chance of her being hunted or shot, that was quite a different matter. The lady was going to see that nobody harmed that fox. She loved it about, and it was not doing any harm to anyone.

She told us how Jenny had appeared that first day and how she had walked into the yard as if she owned it. She had shown no fear of the dogs, but the dogs seemed frightened of her and would not go near the food until Jenny had eaten as much as she wanted. She had not been in any hurry to go. She had sat down and washed herself and had a look round. Then, suddenly, she had leaped right over the fence and made off towards the woods, the same woods in which we had let her go. We saw quite clearly now how she reached the house, for, although it was a good four miles by the road, it could not have been much more than half that distance across the fields.

After that, Jenny went regularly every evening to the yard. She was so punctual that you could have set your clock by her. Lots of people did go up and watch her but they had to stand well back. She accepted dogs but she would not have people near her. Even the lady who fed her had to stand well back and watch from behind the curtain. If strangers were about, the fox would retreat the way she had come and not return until the coast was clear.

She came by the same route each time. We went up one evening to see her coming in for her food. There were a couple more people waiting near the gate, and they told us that they came down frequently to see her, she was such a magnificent animal. She was too. She appeared at the edge of the wood at the exact moment they had told us to expect her. She trotted up to the top of the slope, sat down and looked around her. It was ten past nine on a late summer evening. The sun was sinking beneath the horizon and the colours were losing their brightness.

Jenny stood up, then gambolled across the top of the field. She was silhouetted against the skyline. As she moved, every hair on her body seemed to catch the failing rays of the sun, which lit up the bright red brown of her coat. She looked so proud as she ran, with her head held high and her brush flowing out behind her.

'Jenny, Jenny,' I called, and whistled as I always did when I wanted her to come.

She turned and looked towards me, but there was no recognition in her eyes. She continued trotting along as if we did not exist. We meant nothing to her any more. I felt sad. She had meant a lot to me, but I had only been an incident in her life.

Fred had forgotten us as well, but that was different. The people who had taken her had made a real pet of her. Now she lived as one of the family in the same way that many dogs or cats do, except that she never went out of the house. The people who had her had grown so fond of her they did not like to let her out of their sight. Later on they fenced part of the garden so that she had the run of the house and garden. Dad said she could have jumped the fence if she had wanted to but she seemed to know when she was well off.

In the autumn Fred's scent glands developed. You could smell fox before you got to the gate. The owners asked the vet to remove her scent glands, which he did in a simple operation. Dad said it was not the real answer because Fred would be handicapped if she ever did go wild. Foxes' scent plays an important part in their behaviour towards one another in the wild. That is not likely to arise yet awhile, for Fred seems very happy where she is.

So does Jenny. We often hear about her and know that she is fending for herself as only a fox with Jenny's disposition could. If you hear of a fox that climbs a tree and watches the hunt go by beneath her on Tuesdays and Fridays (hunt days) you can be sure that is Jenny. As Mum said, she had enough practice climbing about the linen cupboard when she was young.

Once when a strange dog chased her, Jenny jumped through an open window into a house. There she sat in an easy chair by the fire, while the surprised elderly couple, whose after-dinner nap she had disturbed, were left to chase the dog away. As soon as it had gone, Jenny walked out of the front door and down the path as if she behaved like that every day.

Mum had worried a bit when they started hunting in the village where Jenny had taken up residence, and she went up there once or twice. There had not been a sign of the fox until Mum went through the village on her way to collect an injured heron. She knew the hunt was out, because she had heard the horn as she came past the wood and she had seen all the horse vans parked outside the farm. All the same, she was not prepared to meet a fox coming along the road. She stopped and watched. The fox stopped and sat down in the middle of the lane, taking time off to have a wash. Then the hounds appeared and the fox stood up, shook herself and trotted farther down the lane without any sign of concern. The hounds seemed to be gaining on her, but she did not quicken her pace. Mum kept up with them, thinking the fox did not have a chance. The hounds were in full cry, and she could hear huntsmen approaching and the horses' hoofs pounding on the tarmac

road. The call of the hunting horn echoed along the lane, and sounds of shouting drew steadily nearer.

The fox did not hurry but trotted right through a group of people who seemed so surprised they did not move. Then she swung into the drive of the poultry farm, slowing down a bit to make sure the hounds were following. With complete ease the fox half-sprang, half-clambered over into the first run and ran across to the next. The first hounds clambered steadily after her, bringing down the wire and tumbling over one another as they did.

Immediately, absolute pandemonium broke out. Chickens were everywhere. They had started to panic as soon as the first dog appeared. Some had crowded into one corner, while others had broken out through the wire and were flying between the horses that had followed the hounds into the yard. The farmer dashed out of his house as soon as he realized what was happening. He only added to the confusion by trying to turn the hounds back and get the hunt out of his yard. Two of the dogs did not help. They had forgotten the fox altogether and were having great fun chasing the hens. Meanwhile the fox had sprung across to the next chicken run and then the next. Several hounds still managed to keep on her tail, and two were able to keep with her right to the eighth and last run. They caused the same panic and confusion in each run as they had in the first one.

The farmer was going crazy by this time, and the hunt followers had left their cars or dismounted from their horses and were trying to restore order. Mum said she had never seen such a mess. Fences were half-down and every corner seemed to be a mixture of frantic hens and hounds. As for the fox, she seemed to be the only one who was not a bit concerned by it all. She climbed out of the last pen and sat at the end, watching everything that was going on. Mum said she looked a picture sitting there with her head cocked a little to one side, looking pert and intelligent. Then the fox stood up and shook herself and trotted off across the fields without a backward glance. Mum was sure it was Jenny.

It was the end of the hunt for that day. It took them the rest of the day to sort the mess out, and I believe the hunt had to pay the farmer a lot of money to compensate him for the damage that had been done.

Jenny led the hunt a dance in November too. The children in the village were getting ready for Bonfire Night, and were building a huge bonfire on the village green. They were building it in the usual way, rather like a wigwam, so that on the day they could fill the centre up with dry paper and sticks so it would be sure to burn. They were really working hard on it when the hunt approached the village. The children stopped to watch. 'Look,' said one of them, pointing along the lane.

There, trotting towards them, was the fox that the hunt had disturbed. She did not seem to be in any hurry. She trotted right past the children and into the middle of the bonfire. When she got there, she curled up and went to sleep. The children stood and stared at her, and then turned to look at the hunt coming along the road.

'I'm not going to let them hurt her,' one of the boys said, and he stood right in front of the bonfire so that the men on horseback could not see the animal behind them. The others agreed and they stood in line too. The huntsmen called the hounds in and asked the children if they had seen the fox, but they shook their heads. All day, the hunt rode round the village, and several times the hounds led them back to the village green. All the time the fox stayed curled up inside the bonfire and the children went on building around it. When the huntsmen broke for the day and started to put their horses into the horse vans, the fox stood up, shook herself, walked out of her hiding place, then continued her journey as if she had not been interrupted.

Jenny is still about. If you go down towards Syston you

might see her. There is no mistaking her for any other fox, because she is easily the most magnificent animal I have ever seen. She has not been seen for three weeks now, and we are wondering if she has cubs of her own. She was certainly seen running with a dog fox earlier in the year. Maybe some day we will see her family.